FATAL FEBRUARY

FATAL FEBRUARY

A Novel

BARBARA LEVENSON

Oceanview Publishing

IPSWICH, MASSACHUSETTTS

ISBN: 978-1-933515-52-6

Published in the United States by Oceanview Publishing, Ipswich, Massachusetts
www.oceanviewpub.com

10 9 8 7 6 5 4 3 2 1

PRINTED IN THE UNITED STATES OF AMERICA

To my husband, Bob Levenson,
without whose love and encouragement,
this book would not have been written.

ACKNOWLEDGMENTS

The places in this book are real while the stories and characters are fictitious.

The criminal justice system in Miami-Dade County, Florida, continues to work against almost insurmountable budget and building restraints. I must acknowledge the background material for this book that comes from working with the courageous judges, attorneys, police, and corrections officers who make the system continue to operate.

I also acknowledge the interesting and diverse people who live and work in the Greater Miami area that has made living here for the past thirty-two years exciting and never boring.

Thanks to Dr. Pat Gussin for her medical input and for her editing and belief in this book and to everyone at Oceanview Publishing.

Last, but certainly not least, to Ned, one of a long line of champion German shepherd dogs from our kennel, who is the model for Sam in this book.

FATAL FEBRUARY

CHAPTER ONE

Lillian Yarmouth murdered her husband. She stabbed him with her grandmother's antique silver letter opener. Right in the heart. At least, that's what everyone in Miami believed, including the *Miami Herald*, although they used the term "allegedly" several times.

She had just come home from the grocery store and the car wash. She was preparing for her son and daughter to return from college for the winter semester break. The kids hated it when she picked them up in her Lexus SUV and it was covered with dust and the leavings of garden plants.

The Yarmouth's next door neighbor, Cassie Kahn, was sunning by her pool. She claimed that she saw Lillian drive into her garage around 3 p.m. She noticed this because the car was so shiny. A short time later, she saw a young, blonde woman run down the street screaming. The woman entered a red BMW parked in front of the Hernandez house. Cassie noticed this because she knew the Hernandez's were in Freeport and she wondered who was at their house.

The police arrived shortly thereafter. They found the upstairs master suite in disarray. Gary Yarmouth's dead body was spread across the king-size bed. Blood stains covered the expensive peach silk coverlet.

The neighbors who had gathered on their front lawns in the toney Coconut Grove neighborhood saw the police lead Lillian away in handcuffs.

CHAPTER TWO

Last February I went to the car wash, and ruined my life. It was the same car wash that my new client, Lillian Yarmouth, had gone to, right before she was accused of murdering her husband.

My name is Mary Magruder Katz. I live in Coral Gables, a suburb of Miami. I'm a lawyer. My main practice is criminal defense, but at the time of Lillian's arrest, I was practicing in a fancy multipartner firm and dabbling in civil and corporate work when I was forced to do so.

A trip to the car wash was a regular monthly occurrence. Nothing special. I was on my way home from work. I knew I was overdue to wash my Ford SUV. The dust of winter in Miami clung to her sides and back window. The beauty of the dry season brings hibiscus blooms, golden shower trees, model photo shoots on South Beach, movie star sightings at restaurants, and eternal sunshine. It also brings yellow Sahara dust that blows across the ocean and clings to cars, patio furniture, and windows.

I should have known Wash 'n' Shine would be

overflowing with dirty cars right before Valentine's weekend. It's a big deal in Miami. It coincides with President's Day weekend, a big tourist time. For the locals, it's also a time to reap the reward of living in South Florida: perfect weather, fun events, and envy from northern relatives.

The line snaked and shimmied up to the vacuum hoses. I left the SUV in the hands of an attendant who appeared to be drunk, drugged, or mentally ill, as he mumbled to himself in unintelligible whispers. The crowd around the viewing windows was deep; children quarreling over a spot to watch their car get its bath, parents yelling, and people chattering in English, Spanish, and Spanglish.

I edged my way to the waiting room to pay for the wash. Just as I put my money down, a tall guy shoved in front of me waving his credit card.

"Excuse me, sir, I was here first."

"Well, I'm in a hurry." He threw the card at the girl behind the counter.

"Hi, Mr. Martin. Good to see you," the girl said

"Look, sir, I was here first." I wedged my body closer to the counter, but it was no use. The big guy reached right over my head and grabbed his bill, signed the slip and threw it back over my head to the cashier.

"Just because you know him, doesn't mean you can be rude to me, miss. And you, Mr. Martin, is that what she called you? Your lack of courtesy is what gives Miami a bad rap."

I paid my bill and walked outside to the waiting area, a large patio with a coffee bar and loud music, basic amenities everywhere in South Florida

There were dozens of cars in an assembly line of attendants who were drying, polishing, and finishing the "instant" car wash. I found a seat on one of the benches and opened my briefcase. It would be a half hour before I could drive out into the growing traffic on the highway.

Loud voices intruded. I could hear them over the music. I looked up and saw the big guy. He was waving his arms at one of the men.

"I said get my car finished *now*. I've told you in English and Spanish. Are you deaf?"

"No, mister, I heard you, but I gotta do these cars in order or I'll lose my job," the attendant said.

"Maybe I'll see that you lose your job anyway."

The attendant took his load of towels and continued through the line of dripping cars.

Ha, I thought, *so you found someone you couldn't bully. Good.*

I looked up from my work when I heard the loudspeaker calling out finished cars.

"White Corvette, your car is ready. Red Ford Explorer, your car is ready."

Only twenty minutes had passed. I was lucky.

I got in my car, readjusted the mirrors, and began to pull slowly out of the drive. I was waiting to enter the traffic flow, when I felt a terrible jolt. My head snapped back. I heard a crunch of metal. Behind me was the white Corvette. Its front was now accordion pleated. I jumped from my car. The driver of the Corvette was getting out. I hurried to look at my car. The back bumper had a small dent and a scratch. Thank God I had opted for an SUV. When I looked up, I was looking into the face of the same Mr. Martin.

"You again," I screamed. "What were you thinking? On your cell phone, I suppose. You're not only rude, you're a self-centered jerk."

"I'm sorry. Look, your car is hardly damaged. Mine is the one that's a mess. I really am sorry." He pulled a stack of bills from his pocket. "Here's five hundred bucks. That should more than cover that little dent. My insurance'll pay for my car, so let's just forget this whole thing."

"Oh, no. Who do you think you are? I'm a lawyer, and I know better than to let you walk away from an accident that's your fault. What if I find I've been injured? My head hurts already. I better call the police."

"Please, don't do that. I know I was wrong. It's just that I've got a big business deal that I've got to get to. Look, here's my card. If there are other damages, I'll pay for them. You can call me."

I looked at the card. Carlos Martin, Developer, Commercial and Residential.

"Yeah, well, half of Miami says they're in the development business. How do I know that's even your real name or number? And if you're going to some big deal, why did you waste time at a car wash?"

"Because I didn't want to show up in a muddy car from a construction site, not that it's any of your business. Here, look, here's my driver's license. It shows my name. Wait, did you say you're a lawyer? Are you busy right now? Do you do real estate closings?"

"Yes, I've done some real estate matters, but actually criminal defense is my specialty."

"Even better. Can you come with me to the closing of this deal? Just look over the contract and the closing statement."

"What? You were rushing off to close a big deal and you don't even have an attorney?"

"Well, I do, but it's the long weekend, and he left with his girlfriend on his boat. Something about trying to sell it at the boat show in Miami Beach. He asked me to put this off, but I can't."

"Well, where's your meeting?"

"It's in Coral Gables. Not far. Only a few minutes from here."

"Nothing in Miami is a few minutes on a Friday afternoon. What about my fee? You haven't even asked what my fee will be."

"Okay, I'll write you a check right now for a thousand dollars, and you can charge me whatever else you think is fair after the meeting. And one more thing. I'm pretty sure my car won't run. It's really smashed. Can you drive me there?"

CHAPTER THREE

Carlos was in the passenger seat of my Explorer before I knew what was happening. His long frame filled the area, even with the seat pushed back. I glanced at him out of the corner of my eye. He was cute, now that he wasn't having a tantrum. I guessed him to be about my age, mid-thirties.

He caught my glance and smiled at me. The smile changed his face. It made him look like a cross between Ricky Martin and Rocky Rothstein. Rocky was the quarterback on my high school football team. I always was a fan of muscles and Latin charisma.

"I don't even know your name." He laughed.

"It's Mary Katz," I said. "I can't take my hands off the wheel to shake hands."

"I think we've met before. You look familiar, and I think I recognize your name, too."

"What a pathetic line. Can't you come up with something more original?"

"No, wait. I'm not conning you. I saw your name

and picture in the paper. Just the other day, but I don't remember what it was about."

"Well, I was in the *Herald* the other day. I represent Lillian Yarmouth. There was a bond hearing, and I was able to get her out of jail. She's on house arrest with an electronic monitor."

"She's the woman who killed her husband? And you got them to release her?" Carlos gave a low whistle of approval or awe. "I'm impressed. And see, I wasn't giving you a tired old line."

"Lillian is innocent until proven guilty," I said. "Nothing makes me boil more than the public convicting someone after reading a squib in the paper."

I began to think about my first meeting with Lillian. My brother called me the day of Gary's murder. Both of my brothers are also lawyers. Jonathan practices estate planning, and William does corporate and real estate work. My parents can't understand why I think their work is boring.

Jonathan was the lawyer Gary Yarmouth hired to do his will. He was the only lawyer Lillian remembered. When her family called Jonathan, he called me.

"I suppose you heard the TV report about Gary Yarmouth's murder," Jonathan said.

"No, I didn't hear it, but our mother did. She already called to warn me about the dangers of working in Coconut Grove."

"Look, Mary, the cops have arrested his wife,

Lillian. She's at the Women's Detention Center. Their daughter called me. I've been their estate lawyer. I explained this wasn't my field, but I'd see if you could go to the jail and see her. I guess she's very frightened."

"You would be too, if you'd ever seen the Women's Annex. That's what they call it. A better name would be the women's hellhole. I'll get over there this evening during visitor hours, and thanks for the referral."

Not too many neighborhoods scare me, but the Women's Annex is at the top of the list for fright night. It's in a high-crime area, a high-drug area, a high-robbery area. There are always characters hanging around the front of the building. Besides those desperate for a drug fix, there are the spouses and boyfriends of the inmates. They are there to intimidate the family visitors in order to keep the women in line and in fear of them. Many of the women are there because of crimes committed by their boyfriends that they've been pulled into.

I drove into the heavily guarded parking lot at 7 p.m. The guard rolled back the gate in the seven-foot chain-link fence, and, after examining my bar card and picture ID, pointed to a parking place. Before I could park, I heard the heavy gate close behind me. I guessed even the guards were afraid.

The entryway contained a heavy glass window with a microphone for communication and a slot to deposit my ID. No one was at the window, so I pounded loudly and waited. A woman of indeterminable age finally appeared. "Hold your water," she rasped. Even through the heavy glass, I could smell the stale cigarette smoke.

I passed my ID in and filled out the paper she passed back: name, bar number, office address, and the name of inmate, Lillian Yarmouth.

The woman took the paper and chuckled. "We took bets about how long it'd be before she had a high-priced lawyer in here. No public defender for the princess. I think I won the pool. I said it'd only be hours."

She motioned me to the door and pushed the buzzer. I entered and moved to the common room. There were a dozen women seated on couches watching TV. They all turned to stare at me. I smiled and moved toward one of the attorney-client booths surrounding the area. The loudspeaker called "Fourth floor, D wing, bring Lillian Yarmouth down, attorney visit."

Several of the women laughed and whispered. They were an odd collection. Some appeared to be no more than teenagers. Others looked old and tired. Some spoke Spanish and stayed in their own tight circle.

After a fifteen-minute wait, a pale woman of about fifty came out of the elevator, accompanied by a porky looking woman officer. I was sure this was Lillian. She had well cut golden brown hair, the kind of color that can only be achieved by frequent visits to a good salon.

She was wearing the prescribed orange smock, but she still had a look of elegance.

"Lillian?" I asked. I'm Mary Katz, Jonathan's sister. He asked me to come and see you. I'm an attorney, too. I specialize in criminal matters. Would you like to talk with me?"

"Oh, yes," she said, with a sigh of what sounded like relief. "Can you get me out of here?"

"Hey, watch it!" Carlos's voice pulled me back to the present. "You're about to pass right by the building, and you came pretty close to sideswiping that truck."

"You've got a lot of nerve criticizing my driving," I said. "I'm not the one that slammed into the back of your car. Remember?"

We pulled into the garage of one of Coral Gables' high-rise office towers.

"Carlos, you better tell me a little about what we're here for. Do you have the paperwork for the closing?"

"Yes, I've got everything in my briefcase, even the cashier's check for the full amount. This is for some land downtown in the Overtown area, several acres. The people who own it got it from the estate of their parents years ago. It has some old rental properties on it."

"What's the closing amount?"

"Five million. I gave them one million as the down payment."

"Six million? For rundown property? What kind of a hot deal is that?"

"Believe me, I know what I'm doing. I've lived in Miami all my life. I don't need investment advice. I just need to make sure the deal goes through and all the paperwork is in order."

We took the elevator up to the offices of Simpson, Carlyle, and Cohen. I was familiar with the firm. They do probate work. I was surprised to see Jim Clark waiting for us in the conference room. We were law school classmates at the University of Miami. His clients were an older man and woman.

Jim and I hugged and exchanged the "I can't believe how long it's beens." His clients were Lois and Lawrence Feller, a brother and sister who had inherited the property. The Feller name was well known. They were benefactors of the opera and ballet. I recognized them from the society pages of the *Herald*.

Carlos pulled out a set of papers and handed them to me. I passed copies of them to Jim. We began to read.

"These papers are all dated last week," Jim said.

"I'm just filling in for Mr. Martin's regular attorney. Let me have a minute with my client."

I leaned over and whispered to Carlos. "What's the story?"

"No story. We were supposed to close last week, but it got postponed," Carlos whispered back.

"Jim, it seems the first closing was postponed. The papers were prepared for that date. It doesn't matter. This is a simple transaction. Only two sellers and one buyer. Let's just get it done now, so we can all enjoy this weekend. If we hurry, the Fellers can get this check over to their bank before they close at six."

"I know nothing about a postponement," Jim said. The Fellers shook their heads.

"Well, Mr. Martin's regular attorney is unavailable. He probably has the explanation. If we can't conclude this deal this afternoon, Mr. Martin may change his mind. Are you sure your clients want to risk losing six million dollars for this property? Who knows when they can find another buyer," I said.

Carlos looked at me and smiled broadly. I was really beginning to like that smile.

"Give me a minute with my clients." Jim walked around the table and led the Fellers into the corner of the room. A vigorous conversation concluded, and they came back to the table.

"I'll get copies made right away, and we can all start signing the originals," Jim said. We all smiled.

"You were great in there," Carlos said as we emerged from the elevator. "How about I buy you a drink next door at the St. Michele."

"Well, okay, but just a quick one. I need to make a phone call to my fiancé."

I pulled out my cell phone and dialed. His voice mail answered.

"Frank, I've been delayed. I had to take care of some matters for a new client. Leave me a message at home about dinner and where to meet."

We settled in at a small table in the French bistro. Carlos ordered Scotch and water and I ordered a glass of Chardonnay. The waiter brought a tray of hors d'oeuvres.

"So," Carlos said, "you have a fiancé. How long have you been engaged?"

"Five years," I said.

"Five years? That's not an engagement, that's a cop-out."

Carlos turned on that sexy smile again. I had to laugh, partially to cover my embarrassment. Carlos is right, I thought.

"Don't you want to get married? Or is he the foot-dragger?"

"I think it's both of us. We have a comfortable relationship, and I work for his law firm. What about you? Are you married?"

"I was, but it didn't last long, not even long enough to think about kids."

"Do you miss her?"

"Oh, no. When people ask me if I've ever had depression, I tell them, no, I got rid of her."

We both laughed.

"Listen, Mary, I need you to get the deed from today's closing recorded as soon as the courthouse opens Monday."

"Monday? Monday's a holiday. It'll have to be Tuesday. What's the rush?"

"I'll explain it at another time. I know I've kept

you too long, but I would like you to represent me again in another matter. I have an Israeli investor coming in town Monday, and there'll be another deal to close. I was impressed with how tough you were today."

"Well, thanks, Carlos. Here's my card. My office is in Coconut Grove. Call me."

I gathered my briefcase and started toward the door.

"Hey, wait," Carlos yelled. "How am I getting home?"

"That's what taxis are for."

CHAPTER FOUR

The next morning was the beginning of the world-famous Coconut Grove Art Show. It's the largest outdoor show in the country. Visitors come from all over the Americas to view art, listen to music, and sample international cuisine. The show begins with a breakfast for patrons and art collectors at 7 a.m., followed by a walk through the show before it opens to the public. Frank and I have attended for five years, and I have gone to the show since I was a teenager. This year the show coincided with Frank's annual golf outing in Palm Beach with his law school buddies from Harvard.

Franklin Fieldstone never tires of reminding everyone in the firm that he was a Harvard law graduate. I knew he had been near the bottom of his class. Yes, I snooped through his records one day when he was out. I graduated second in my class. So, my question is, would you rather be represented by the top of the class from Miami, or the guy who scraped through at Harvard?

I rolled out of bed at six, fed my dog, Sam, threw on jeans, a tee shirt, and sandals, and hit the road for the breakfast. I was filling my plate and trying to balance my coffee cup, when a hand took my elbow, and grabbed the cup.

"May I be of assistance?" a male voice said. I recognized the voice.

"Carlos, what are you doing here?" I realized I was pleased.

"I'm a patron, just like you. I come every year. I think I remember seeing you here last year. Weren't you wearing a cute straw sun hat? And where is the famous Frank?"

"The hat's over there. I left it on my table. Frank is unavailable today."

"That's not your table. Come with me."

He didn't wait for an answer. He took my plate and proceeded to a reserved table with the main sponsors of the show. MARTIN DEVELOPMENT was printed on the gold sponsor board next to the table.

"Can we walk through the show together?" he asked, as people began to leave the tables.

"Sure." I put on the straw hat and wondered why I felt so happy.

There were artists I've gotten to know over the years, and I stopped frequently to tell an artist where her or his picture was hanging, and to admire their new work. Carlos bought a large canvas of a tropical scene.

"You need a big wall for that," I said.

"I have several to cover. I built a house last year in Pinecrest. It wasn't selling at the price I wanted, so I moved into it. I'm glad, because the prices are escalating, and meanwhile I like the house. Every time I come home I say 'Carlos, you're a damn good builder.' Where do you and Frank live?"

"Oh, we don't live together. I have a house in Coral Gables with a yard for my dog. Frank has a condo on Brickell Key, overlooking the bay. He likes to look at the water. I like my little house, so he stays with me sometimes and I stay with him sometimes, but I'm not willing to give up my house."

"What kind of dog do you have? What's his name?"

"He's mostly German shepherd. His name is Uncle Sam, because I found him as an abandoned puppy on the Fourth of July six years ago. He only weighed about ten pounds. He looked like a tiny bear cub. Now he weighs eighty pounds."

We walked and talked. Carlos insisted on buying me a pair of earrings I tried on. He said it was a down payment on the next legal matter.

The crowds began to grow as the morning wore on. I spotted a familiar face moving toward us.

"Mary, I thought that was you. Where's Frank?" It was Karl Morris, the prosecutor assigned to Lillian's case. He stared at Carlos, who had his arm around my shoulder.

"Frank's at a golf outing. Let me introduce Carlos

Martin. Mr. Martin is a developer. I'm doing some legal work for him."

The two men shook hands and eyed each other like two male dogs at the dog park.

"I guess we'll be seeing a lot of each other in the next few months," Karl said. "The Yarmouth case is a top priority at my office. We've already assigned two other prosecutors to work on it."

"So I guess that means it'll take three of you to handle Mary's defense," Carlos said. He smiled at Karl, but it looked more like a smirk.

"Well, Karl, it's good to see you out of the court-room. I'll call you next week. I want discovery imme-diately, and I plan to start depositions as soon as I can get subpoenas served. Talk to you next week," I said, as I pulled Carlos by the arm and marched away.

"If you've got time maybe we can have lunch and talk about the deal I'm involved in next week," Carlos said, as we reached the end of the show.

"I guess I could. Or is this just so I can drive you around this afternoon? How did you get here? How's the Corvette?"

"I had the Corvette towed to the dealer. I have my Escalade here today."

I laughed to myself. Two years ago the car of choice for the in-crowd was an Expedition, but last year the Hummer and the Escalade were the accepted status cars. Who knows? Maybe next year we'll all drive tanks.

I left my car in the parking garage and climbed into the Escalade. Carlos drove over the causeway to Key Biscayne. The day was a perfect tourist ad. The water was aquamarine, the sky was an endless blue ceiling, the temperature a balmy seventy-two, according to the dashboard thermometer. Cruise ships were parked in the port across the bay. I wondered when I had last taken the time to enjoy my surroundings.

We pulled up to a small restaurant and opted to sit on the patio facing the water. Carlos ordered a pitcher of sangria. We sat and drank and watched the boats pass and smelled the scent of the sea. Carlos didn't mention his new business deal, and I admit, I didn't ask. I was too relaxed.

"What kind of a name is Mary Katz?" he asked

"A Miami kind of name. My full name is Mary Magruder Katz. My mother's family was Southern Baptist. Her father brought the family here when she was a kid. He was the education director at that old downtown church. My dad's family owned Katz's Kosher Market on Miami Beach. My mom and dad met on the beach one weekend when they were teenagers, and that's how I got my name. The Magruder was my mother's maiden name."

Carlos laughed.

"What's so funny? Your name is pretty mixed up too."

"I guess so. My mother came with her family from Cuba, long before Castro took over. Her father was hired as a professor at the university, and they never went back. My father came here from Argentina to go to college. We think his family came from Germany, but no one will say whether they were escaping the Nazis or whether they were the Nazis."

"Well, I guess neither of us will ever need sensitivity training in diversity." I glanced at my watch. "Carlos, it's three o'clock, and we haven't discussed your new legal matter. This isn't conducive for a business meeting. Why don't we go back to my office? It's in the Grove and you'll have to take me back to my car anyway."

That simple suggestion turned out to be fatal.

CHAPTER FIVE

We arrived at my office. All was quiet. I turned on my desk lamp and we settled on either end of my large leather sofa.

"Tell me about this Israeli investor," I said.

"Actually, he's coming to purchase the property I bought yesterday." Carlos looked out the window as he spoke.

"You mean you're going to propose a sale to him?

"Not exactly. He's already given me a deposit, and I have a rough draft of the papers to transfer owner- ship to him. That's why I need the deed recorded im- mediately."

"What were you thinking? You sold property you didn't own. That's fraud. That's a crime."

"Well, I own it now. All you have to do is get the deed recorded. The papers have the earlier closing date. Remember?"

"You lied to me, and you're making me a part of this crime. I could lose my license to practice law. How could you do this?"

Carlos moved across the sofa, and put his arm around me. "Ah, *mi amor,* please, don't be angry with me."

"I am not your love," I shouted.

"You think not?" Carlos said, and he pulled me close and kissed me.

The next thing I knew I was kissing him back. One thing led to another and a few minutes later we were lying entwined on my leather sofa with our clothes strewn on the desk, the computer, and the floor. I couldn't believe what had just happened. I also couldn't believe how happy I felt, happier than I'd been in years. I had just lived every woman's fantasy. You know, meeting some hot stranger in an elevator and having sex with him between floors.

Dusk was falling outside, and I was feeling sleepy from the sangria. A sudden noise startled me. The outer office door opened and I heard Frank.

"Mary, are you here?" My office door flew open. "What are you doing at work?" Frank spoke before he focused in the dim light. "Oh, my God. I guess I can see what you're doing."

Carlos was up grabbing his clothes. I remember asking him to leave. I grabbed my shirt and sat eyeing Frank.

"Is that guy a client?" Frank asked.

"He's sort of a client."

"Mary, don't you realize this whole office could be

in trouble with the bar? There's an ethics rule that pro-hibits sexual acts with a client."

"Is that what's upsetting you?" I asked. "Just that the office could suffer? You don't really care about me, do you? I guess we should have faced the fact long ago that this was a business engagement, not a love en-gagement. Well, you're off the hook. Here's your ring," I said, as I removed the two-karat diamond. "And an-other thing, I quit your law practice, too."

"Good," Frank said, "because you're fired, and don't think you can steal a bunch of my clients."

"Your clients. I've brought in all my own clients, and you know it."

Frank slammed the door as he strode out. I put on the rest of my clothes and began filling boxes and bags with my belongings. I copied the contents of my computer, grabbed my files, and began making trips to my car. In retrospect, I think I liked the two-karat di-amond a lot better than I liked Frank, because I missed the ring immediately.

CHAPTER SIX

I was seated in my living room on Sunday morning. Boxes of office stuff filled the hallway. Sam and I were lolling on the sofa feeling sorry for ourselves. I had a mug of coffee and the unopened *New York Times* in my lap. Sam had his favorite tennis ball. I must have looked as sad as I felt in my old terry bathrobe and sneakers, when the doorbell rang.

"Who is it?" I yelled. Sam bounded back and forth waiting for the door to open. He loves company.

"It's Carlos."

"Go away," I said. "How did you find my house?"

"Open the door and I'll tell you."

Curiosity won out, and I opened the door. Sam put his paws on Carlos's shoulders and licked his face. Carlos rubbed Sam's ears and chest. An instant bond of friendship was forged.

"Can I come in?" Carlos asked, as he moved through the door. "Haven't you heard of the Internet? I Googled you. Got your address, phone number, social security number, credit rating, which was only fair;

everything but your bra size, but I already knew that."

I was not in the mood for jokes. "What do you want?"

"I want to find out if you're okay. I see you're not wearing the rock engagement ring. Is that over?"

"Of course, my engagement is over and I am now out of job. That's my office sitting around in these boxes."

"This is not a worry. I have a building on Dixie Highway. There are many lawyers in the building. I will rent you an office immediately."

"What's the rent?"

"Whatever you want to pay."

"Don't think this will allow you to have sex with me again," I said.

"The office space has nothing to do with that. I was hoping you would want to have sex with me because you liked it."

On Monday morning, I was moving into my new office. I insisted on paying a thousand bucks and gave Carlos back his check as payment.

On Tuesday, I recorded the deed to the Overtown property. Carlos had a friend in the clerk's office who accommodated an instant recording. On Wednesday, I met with Carlos and the Israeli. It turned out that the investor would only eat kosher cuisine, so I accompanied him to Forty-first Street in Miami Beach where I knew every Kosher restaurant. My grandfather Katz was still remembered fondly. We were treated like celebrities, and by Thursday, Carlos's deal was closed. His six-million-dollar investment was sold for thirty-eight million dollars. Carlos had learned that the whole area was being rezoned for high-rise condos, and the Israeli expected to build seventy-five units to be sold for two million dollars apiece.

I was feeling pretty good with my hefty fees from Carlos and my regular clients transitioning to my new office. Life was good.

Life was good for me, but not for Lillian. Monday evening I phoned her and asked if I could come by and see her. She was not staying in the house in Coral Gables. The police still had it roped off as a crime scene. She had moved to a condo on Miami Beach. Gary had bought it as a rental investment, but it was unoccupied and furnished so Lillian and her son and daughter moved in.

She was wearing an electronic bracelet and could not go farther than the range of the telephone without setting off an alarm. Her two children had refused to leave her and return to school, so they were there to run errands. The court did not even allow Lillian to attend her husband's funeral. House arrest meant just that.

The condo was in one of the high-rise behemoths that cover Collins Avenue, which is called the Concrete Canyon by us natives. Behind the buildings lies the ocean. But an out-of-towner would never know it's there. It is completely hidden by the oversized buildings.

I searched for the address, 5801 Collins. I spotted it looming at the top of a lighted circular drive. I pulled up under the covered entry. A valet parker rushed out to claim my car. He turned up his nose when he viewed the dog hair and half-chewed tennis ball on the passenger seat. The guard in the ornate lobby checked my name off a list and I whisked up on the elevator to the fifteenth floor.

Lillian opened the door, but she appeared to be in shock. She was dressed in a bathrobe. Her hair was uncombed and she was without any makeup, even lipstick. She had turned into an old woman overnight.

She motioned to the living room. Several days' newspapers covered the sofa. She pushed them to the floor and motioned for us to sit.

"Where are your son and daughter?" I asked. "It's Sherry and Brett, right?"

"They're taking a walk on the beach," Lillian said. She remained quiet, her hands in her lap. She didn't meet my gaze.

"Lillian, I'm here for two reasons. We had very little time to talk at the jail, and I need to know everything you can tell me that will help me prepare your case." I pulled a pad and pen from my purse. "But before we even get to that, I need to explain to you that I have left the Fieldstone firm and opened my own

office. Here's my new card with all the numbers and
e-mail so you can reach me at any time."

I paused when I saw Lillian look up with a startled
expression. At least I caught her attention.

"I will still be able to give you full representation,
but it's your decision as to whether you feel comfortable with me as your lawyer under these new circum-
stances."

"Don't you want to be my lawyer?" Lillian asked.
Tears welled up in her red-rimmed eyes.

"Certainly, I do. It's just that I want to be fair to
you and be sure that being in a small office rather than
a large firm doesn't make you uncomfortable in any
way."

"I like you, Mary. I hired you. I don't know anything about law offices. I just need help." She began to
sob.

I pulled a wad of Kleenex from my purse and put
it in her lap. "I'm here to help, but I need you to help
yourself, as well. Remember when we talked at the jail?
You told me what you wanted was to go home and take
a shower and wash your hair. As soon as you and I finish talking, that's what I want you to do; shower, do
your hair, put on some slacks and some makeup. You
need to do it for yourself and for your kids. Now
let's start talking about you and everything you can
remember about the day Gary died."

She dabbed at her eyes with the Kleenex. "I was so
happy that day. Sherry and Brett were on their way

home from Dartmouth. They were going to be here for five days, to thaw out they said. Gary was going to be home early to go with me to the airport. I went to the grocery and then to get the car washed. I pulled into the garage and saw that Gary's car was already there. I pulled a couple of grocery bags out and went through the garage door into the back hall. I thought I heard the front door or some noise. I called for Gary, but there was no answer. I went up the back stairs and into his office. He wasn't there, so I went into our bedroom and I saw all the blood and him." She stopped abruptly. Her face was ashen and she began to shake violently.

"Lillian, are you okay?" I put her feet up on the sofa and forced her to stretch out. I went to the bedroom and found a quilt, which I threw over her. I found the kitchen, ransacked the cupboards until I found a bottle of brandy. I rushed back to the living room and forced her to drink a few sips of the brandy. Lillian was clearly in shock.

"Who is your doctor?" I shouted. I wasn't sure she could hear me. "Have you been prescribed any medications to help you through this time?"

She looked at me, her eyes glassy. "It's Dr. Gordon," she mumbled.

The door opened and two young people came in.

"Mother," the young woman rushed over to the sofa. "Who are you?" she looked angrily at me.

"I'm Mary Katz, your mother's attorney. You're Sherry and Brett?"

"Oh, hi," Sherry said. Brett extended his hand. "What happened?"

I drew the two of them into the hall and explained that I was sure their mother was in shock and needed medical help.

"Can you call her doctor? I need her to get back on her feet so she can help prepare her case. And I need both of you to come to my office as soon as possible. I'll need your input, anything you can tell me about your dad. Call and make appointments as soon as possible." I thrust my card into Brett's hand. "Please, call me later tonight or tomorrow and let me know how your mother's doing." I let myself out.

CHAPTER SEVEN

On the following Monday, as I arrived at the office, I was greeted by Luis, the process server we used at Frank's office.

"Hi, Luis, what are you doing here? Slumming?"

"No, Ms. Katz, sorry, consider yourself served." He thrust papers at me.

I was stunned. I opened the folder and found that Frank was suing me for the theft of trade secrets and business interference. The vindictive son of a bitch wanted a temporary restraining order for allegedly stealing his clients.

I was shaking when I entered the office. The receptionist in the law office across the hall called to me. She was answering my phone until I could hire an assistant.

"Ms. Katz, the Florida Bar has been calling you all morning. You need to call them right back."

My first thought was that I hadn't updated my new address. I dialed the number that answered, "Florida

Bar Ethics Commission." I hung up and shut my office door.

I looked through the rest of my messages. There was one from Katy Levine, a law-school buddy who works as counsel to the Florida Bar. I dialed her number. She took the call immediately.

"Hi, Katy, what's up?"

"Mary, I wanted to give you a heads up. I happened to see an ethics complaint that was filed last Friday. It'll probably be delivered to you today. I couldn't believe it."

"Believe what?"

"Franklin Fieldstone has filed a complaint about you having sexual relations with a client. I thought you and he were engaged. What's going on?"

"It's a long story. Thanks for going out on a limb to let me know. I'll tell you all when this is over."

The room was whirling. I put my head down on my desk. I had never been sued in my life and I had a flawless bar record, not even one complaint from a client, not even the ones serving life sentences. In a matter of minutes, my record was smashed. I needed help. When my clients are in trouble, what's my first piece of advice? "You need a lawyer." I racked my brain. Who could handle this whole mess?

I thumbed through the rest of my phone messages. The top one was from the law school. They needed help with an alumni project. Bang! That was it. My favorite law professor, Karen Kominsky. She was an institution in South Florida. An authority on commercial law and a former member of the board of governors of the bar, and an advocate for women. I dashed to my car and headed for the campus.

CHAPTER EIGHT

On the way back to the office, I realized that I hadn't bothered to look at the rest of my phone messages. My own problems were starting to interfere with my client's problems. Professor Kominsky was going to work on my case. I had to turn my attention to my clients.

I called the office from my cell phone. The line rang eight times before the receptionist across the hall picked up. I hadn't had time to start interviewing for an assistant. I was going to have to make time. The other lawyers in the building were gracious about offering help with my phone, but I needed a person of my own.

"Ms. Katz's office," a vague-sounding voice finally answered.

"Hi, it's Mary Katz, just checking in."

"Who?" the voice answered.

"Me, the person whose phone you just answered. Are there any messages for me?"

"Oh, just the ones I gave you before."

"So there's nothing new for me?"

"Well, yes, there's a young girl sitting in your office. Sherry something? Said you wanted to see her."

"Oh, my God. How long has she been there?"

"Oh, maybe fifteen minutes. I guess I told her she could come over when she called before."

"Heather, that's your name isn't it? You never checked to see if I was there. How could you give her an appointment?"

"Yes, Heather's my name. Listen, we're pretty busy here. I can't run around looking for you."

"Okay, never mind, just go across the hall and tell her I'll be right there." I slammed the cell phone against the steering wheel. Damn Frank Fieldstone and Carlos Martin and everyone else that was messing up my life.

I broke all the speed limits and raced from the parking lot into my office. Sherry Yarmouth was sitting on the sofa. She had a book open in her lap, but she didn't appear to be reading. She was staring out the window. She looked a lot like her mother. She had a certain air of fashion even dressed in jeans, a Dartmouth tee shirt, and flip-flops.

"Sherry, thanks for coming over. I'm so sorry I was detained at another appointment."

"It's okay. I really don't have much to do right now except take care of Mother. I'm used to being so busy at school. Everything is just so weird."

"Will you and your brother stay out of school this term?"

"We haven't decided. I'm trying to keep up-to-date with my reading in case we do go back. Right now, I can't think about much except missing my dad and — everything. Can you help my mother?"

"I'm sure going to try my best. I haven't been able to have a very meaningful interview with your mother yet. How is she today?"

"Not much better. Dr. Gordon called in a prescription for her. It's to help her sleep, which is what she's been doing all day today. She's so depressed." Sherry's voice wavered. She was trying not to cry.

"Tell me about your family. Your parents' relationship."

"That's why this whole thing is so horribly strange," she said. "My parents were devoted to each other. They've been married, I mean were married, twenty-five years. They did a lot of stuff together, traveled, played golf, went out on the boat. It's crazy to think Mom would ever hurt Dad, let alone do what the police said."

"I don't believe I know where your dad worked. What did he do?"

"He and my uncle were in business together, wine distribution. They supplied all the hotels and restaurants."

"How about your mom? Does she work?"

"She's a dedicated homemaker. Never had a career, but she's active in a lot of organizations. Dad always joked that she did more work for her charities than some people did in full-time jobs. I think sometimes she wished she had had a career. She's always encouraging me to be able to support myself. But she went to college, Wellesley. She could have had a career. She came back to Miami. She was born and raised here. Then she met Dad and they got married."

"Was your dad from Miami too?"

"Oh, no, he was born and raised in Brooklyn. He came to Miami on a scholarship. He played football. He was the placekicker."

"Do you know anyone who was mad at your dad? Or anything your parents argued about?"

Well, sometimes they argued about where to go for dinner, or whether Brett and I should go to the same college, but no big things. I don't think Dad had any enemies. I think my uncle was kind of jealous of him. They argued about the business sometimes or family stuff."

"Where's Brett today? I thought he'd be coming with you."

"We didn't want to leave Mom alone for too long, and he said he'd come over by himself."

"Will you ask him to come over soon? How do I get in touch with your uncle?"

"He's trying to keep everything going at work, but

I'll tell him to call you." Sherry pulled herself up from the sofa. She looked so forlorn. Her sad eyes made me think of a wounded puppy.

"I'll call your uncle. What's his name, and where can I reach him?"

"Jack Brandeis. Just call the office, Elite Wine Distributors."

"Sherry, I have one last question. I don't want to upset you, but this is something I need to know. The newspaper said that the weapon used to stab your dad was an antique silver letter opener. Have you ever seen that letter opener?"

"I think so. I think it belonged to my grand-mother."

"Do you know where it was kept?"

"No. Most of our silver was kept in drawers in cloth covers. Mom might have had it in her writing desk in the bedroom. That's where she kept her mail, but I can't really remember seeing it there."

"Okay, Sherry. You've helped me a lot. If you think of anything else, even the smallest detail, please, call me."

I watched Sherry walk across the parking lot and get into an Audi sports car. Something told me that there was a lot about this family that I'd have to dig out. The uncle must be Lillian's brother, not Gary's. I moved to the computer and Googled Elite Wines.

There was a good bit of information that popped up.

Elite Wines: founded 1953 by the late Martin
Brandeis
Current President: Gary Yarmouth
Vice President: Jack Brandeis
Gross sales for 2004: $20,000,000
Largest Clients: The Forge Restaurant, Four
Seasons Hotels South Florida, Ritz Carleton
Hotels South Florida, Omni Hotels nationally

Board of Directors: Lillian Yarmouth, Marian
Brandeis, Angelina Martin, Guillermo Gonzalez

Warehouse and Home Office, 13555
Biscayne Blvd., North Miami, Florida

So Elite was owned by Lillian's family, and I was
right, Jack must be her brother, but he's not the head
honcho. Gary must have beat him out of the presidency.
No wonder Sherry said her uncle was jealous of her dad.

I dialed Elite Wines. "Jack Brandeis, please."

"He's not available. I'll give you his voice mail,"
said a bored female voice.

"No, I need to speak to him directly. It's very important."

"That's not possible. There's been a death in the
family, and he's unavailable."

I thought I heard gum chewing on the other end
of the line. "Look, miss, I know there's been a death
in the family. This is Mary Magruder Katz, Lillian
Yarmouth's attorney. Can't you contact him?"

"Just a minute," the voice said. Boredom had turned to impatience.

While I waited, I printed out the information from the computer. Angelina Martin? Was that a relative of Carlos who was on the board of Elite? A male voice interrupted my thoughts.

"This is Jack Brandeis."

"Mr. Brandeis, this is Mary Katz, your sister's attorney. Lillian is your sister, correct?"

"Yes, Ms. Katz. Just tell me what I can do to help. I guess you're calling about your fee. Of course, the company and I will take care of whatever is necessary."

"No, this isn't about my fee. I'm calling to ask you to come to my office, so we can talk about Lillian's case. Your sister is not able to communicate much. She's very depressed. I need as much information about the family and the business, so I can prepare her defense."

"Well, I'm afraid I'm awfully busy right now. I have to keep things going here. The office is in a turmoil. I'm sure you understand. Maybe next week."

"I understand that you can't get away, so I'll come to your office. Tomorrow. Is morning or afternoon better for you, or shall I pick the time?"

"Come over around noon. I'll do my best to spend a little time with you." He hung up.

I was getting the picture that the Yarmouth-Brandeis clan was not one big happy family.

CHAPTER NINE

My desk was piled high with unanswered motions, un-opened mail, and assorted dirty coffee mugs. I had to hire an assistant. The support staff at my old firm appeared in my memory as perfection, even though I had griped about them. All of the associates believed they spied on us for the partners, but they did keep the wheels of justice moving.

I grabbed my copy of the *Daily Legal Review* and turned to the want ads. One ad jumped off the page. LEGAL SHMEEGLE FOR ALL YOUR LAW OFFICE NEEDS. The name made me giggle, until I read more.

> Margaret Shmeegle, former legal secre-tary at one of America's top-ten law firms, will find the right people to serve your every law office need. Paralegals, secretaries, receptionists, computer spe-cialists, we have them all and they are trained and ready to make your office a perfect Shmeegle experience.

I grabbed the phone, and within minutes Ms. Shmeegle herself promised to send over the perfect candidate first thing the next morning. Brittany Wilson would be there with a résumé filled with experience.

After a few minutes of sorting the haphazard papers on my desk into something that passed for neat piles, I sat back and contemplated the events of the day. My head ached thinking of Frank suing me, and the bar investigating me. I had no clue into Lillian's case, and my other clients' files were untouched. I knew what I needed.

Carlos had given me his cell phone numbers. He carried more than one and also had a satellite phone in the Escalade. The first number I tried answered immediately.

"Mary, is that you? I recognized your number on the caller ID. What's up?"

A great question. I knew what I hoped was up. "I've had a lousy day. How about dinner tonight? I'll pick up something on my way home."

"Hey, you've never seen my house. I'll provide dinner there and maybe even some after dinner entertainment, if you're in the mood," he said.

"I can probably get in the mood," I answered. "Seven o'clock?"

I was definitely in the mood. Why else did he think I called?

*   *   *

I locked up and went straight home, fed Sam, and walked him. I soaked in a bubble bath perfumed with Obsession bath oil. I put on my prettiest undies, a mini skirt, and low-cut blouse, and I was on my way.

Pinecrest is an old suburb filled with enormous ficus and oak trees. All the pines are gone because of some kind of beetles, but the name is still there. There are older homes mixed in with new McMansions. The name of choice this year for these humongous abodes is Starter Castles.

I pulled into the circular drive at the address Carlos gave me. There was a brick courtyard in front of a fake Mediterranean château. Starter Castle was definitely the right name for this one. The doorbell sounded like a call to church. The only outdoor amenity lacking was a moat with a crocodile.

Carlos opened the door. Behind him was a two-story entry hall with a sort of turret at the very top with stained-glass skylights. He was dressed in shorts and a polo shirt. An appetizing odor of cooking wafted from somewhere. I wasn't sure whether it was the food or Carlos that whet my appetite.

He pulled me in the door and kissed me. My headache disappeared.

"Oh, come with me," he said, and pulled me through the hall and into a kitchen, which looked as if it had been designed for a professional chef. Gleaming stainless steel appliances were reflected in the glossy white tile. Cherry cabinets and a refrigerator that looked large enough to walk into filled the walls

"When I saw you, I forgot that I was cooking." He pointed to a bar stool in front of a butcher-block island in the center of the room

I sat down and Carlos put a glass of wine in front of me. "You didn't have to cook," I said. "I had no idea you had so many talents."

"You haven't begun to enjoy my talents yet, but maybe you can start tonight. What happened today that was so lousy?"

"I'm being sued by my ex-boss for stealing his clients and trade secrets. The jerk has gotten an ethics complaint filed against me by the Florida Bar. I had to hire myself a lawyer, and my murder case makes no sense. I also have no help in my office, and I seem to be going in circles."

"What kind of ethics thing?" Carlos looked over at me with a frown.

"The bar has a rule about attorneys having sex with their clients. Frank, the vindictive son of a bitch, filed a complaint about what he saw in the office. You know, you and me."

"Oh, so that's all." Carlos looked relieved. "I thought maybe it had to do with the work you did on the Israeli deal. You'll get past all of this. My grandmother always said 'the smaller the problem, the faster the solution.' Or something like that. It doesn't seem to translate too well. Drink your wine and relax. I have a great shrimp creole cooking." He crossed the room and put an arm around me.

"Carlos, will the food hold for a while? Maybe you could show me the rest of the house and your bedroom."

"Come on," he said, as he turned off the oven.

A few hours later, I felt happy and almost giddy. We had just finished a late dinner, when I remembered something.

"Is Angelina Martin, by any chance, a relative of yours?" I asked.

"She's my mother. Why do you ask? Don't tell me she's in trouble."

"Not that I know of. Does she get in trouble a lot? The reason I asked is that her name came up on the board of directors of Elite Wines. That's the company that Gary Yarmouth was president of. You know, my client's husband that she's accused of offing."

"My parents are on a number of boards. My dad has a few businesses here and in Argentina. I can't keep track of all of them. Maybe you could ask her yourself. They'd love to meet you."

"You mean you mentioned me to your parents?"

"Sort of. I told them I was going to marry you. How about dinner with them this weekend? Or maybe when they go to their beach condo on Marco Island?"

I was stunned. Marriage? Well, he was a keeper, and he could cook.

CHAPTER TEN

The next morning I left Carlos's house at six o'clock and dashed for home. I couldn't go to work in the mini-skirt outfit, and I had abandoned poor Sam.

I came into the house through the kitchen. Sam was nowhere to be seen. No barks greeted me. I went into the living room and found that it had snowed over night. That's how it looked. Sam had punished me for failing to return. He had chewed open the needlepoint pillows my mother had made for the sofa. Stuffing was everywhere. It's amazing how foam shreds into millions of tiny snowflakes.

"Sam. Get out here now," I yelled.

He crawled out from under the dining room table. He was wearing a wreath of needlepoint fabric around his neck. He looked so funny that I couldn't scold him. Instead, I gave him his breakfast, made some coffee, and began to shovel my way through the foam snow.

"Next time, you can go with me. I think you'll love Carlos's big backyard," I said.

*   *   *

I arrived at the office a couple of minutes before nine, and waited to meet Brittany, the Shmeegle-trained assistant. Nine fifteen came and went, but still no Brittany. At nine thirty the door opened and a high voice called out, "Hello? Miss. Uh. Hello?"

As I entered the reception room, a stream of heavy perfume filled my nostrils.

"Brittany? I'm Mary Katz. Please come in." I led her into my office.

She was dressed in jeans so tight they appeared to be painted on her ample behind. With the jeans, she wore a baby-doll top, at least thirty clanking silver bracelets, and high-heeled boots. She had long red hair and long red fingernails.

"Please have a seat." I motioned to the chair across the desk from me. "Did you bring your résumé?"

"Of course." She handed it to me. "I hope Margaret told you that I do not work past five o'clock, and I need to have lunch at twelve every day."

"Why don't I look over your résumé first," I said. "What was the last law firm you worked for?"

"It was the law office of Hank Fowler. It's all right there."

"What was the reason you left there? It doesn't seem to be here." I skimmed down the single page of paper.

"He was disbarred, so there wasn't any more work there." She smiled and looked around the office.

"Where will I be sitting. I absolutely have to have a window where I work. I have claustrophobia." She smiled again.

"That seems to be your only law firm experience. How long were you there?"

"Three months."

"The next place you worked was Stanley's Pest Control. What did you do there?"

"I answered the phones. When customers called up with special problems, like mice in the kitchen or bugs or something, I dispatched a truck to take care of it."

"I see. How long did you work there?"

"Six months, but I quit. Everyone smelled like bug spray. It made me sick."

"Then you were at Mike's Body Shop."

"Yeah, I was the cashier in one of those little window places, where the customers go to pick up their cars, but they get them only if they pay, you know. I had to leave there. The claustrophobia got me."

"I thought Ms. Shmeegle said you were a trained legal secretary."

Well, I worked for Hank and he was a lawyer. When do you want me to start and what's the pay?"

"Somehow, Brittany, I don't think you're right for this job, but thanks for coming over." I stood up and led her to the door. So much for the Shmeegle legal service.

I was back to square one. I dug into the first pile of motions, booted up my computer, and thanked God that I knew how to type.

CHAPTER ELEVEN

I drove into the parking lot of Elite Wines at five minutes before noon for my appointment with Jack Brandeis. The two-story stucco building covered the whole block. The front of the building looked like an office building with floor-to-ceiling glass doors. At the back, near the parking lot, were a loading dock and numerous trucks. I chose the front door. Jack Brandeis didn't sound like the type to be hands-on, shipping and receiving cargo. He sounded like the executive type, consumed with his own importance. He had tried to dodge meeting with me. I was getting the idea he cared more about Elite Wines than about his sister.

An information desk filled the front lobby. Three attractive young women were behind the desk fielding telephone calls. They looked more like models than receptionists. One of the Naomi Campbell look-alikes finally noticed me.

"I have an appointment with Jack Brandeis. I'm Mary Katz." I handed her my card.

I glanced around the lobby. It was decorated in an

art deco look. A showcase was filled with interesting wine bottles. A poster announced the new wine of the month. A sauvignon blanc from New Zealand. Mymind wandered. A bottle of wine and Carlos sure would be great. The receptionist broke into my daydream.

"I'll ring him," she said in a fake British accent, "but I believe he just left the building."

"That can't be correct. We had an appointment for twelve sharp." I tried to swallow the anger building up in my throat. I had left my office at eleven and fought the traffic through the usual freeway lane closings for repairs. I had left loads of other clients' work strewn around my office.

The receptionist was on the phone. "Yes, I told her he went out, but she insists that she has an appointment. Okay, I'll tell her."

She replaced the phone and turned to me. "Mr. Brandeis is very sorry. He was called out unexpectedly and asks that you reschedule."

"That won't be necessary. I'll wait in his office," I said as I rushed for the elevator. I had glanced at the guide as I entered the lobby and noted executive offices, second floor.

I was in the elevator before any of the models could chase me down in their super spike heels. I imagined that they were calling security, but I was dashing down the hallway until I saw the mahogany double doors with a gold plate announcing executive suite.

The woman behind the desk was wiping her

glasses. It was obvious she had been crying. She looked more like a librarian than an executive secretary. Her salt-and-pepper hair was held tightly in a bun. She wore a dark dress and pearls.

"Excuse me." I said. "I'm here to see Jack Brandeis. We have an appointment for twelve o'clock."

The woman looked me over. "They called from the lobby. They said you came up here without permission."

"Look, I'm Lillian Yarmouth's attorney. Mr. Brandeis was unable to come to my office, so I came here to interview him. It's essential that I meet with everyone who can help me with Mrs. Yarmouth's defense."

Before I finished my sentence, the woman began to cry in great gulping sobs. I moved around the desk and patted her shoulder. My handy supply of Kleenex was retrieved from my briefcase. Tears go with the territory of criminal defense.

"I didn't mean to upset you," I said.

"Oh, it's not you. It's just everything that's happened. We all loved Gary — Mr. Yarmouth, and his wife, too. It's so sad here without him. I'm sorry, I'm Beverly Klein, Mr. Yarmouth's administrative assistant. Or I guess I should say, I was his assistant." This brought on a new flood of tears.

"Where is Mr. Brandeis anyway? We were supposed to meet here at noon."

"God knows," she sniffled. "He hightailed it out of here a few minutes ago."

"Well, I'm going to sit right here and wait for him." I marched over to one of the leather easy chairs and plunked down. "You better call downstairs and see if they're sending some security guys up here to evict me. Oh, by the way, I'm Mary Katz. While I'm waiting, why don't you and I talk about Gary and Lillian? Maybe you can give me some help."

Beverly seemed accustomed to following orders. She called off the hounds who were on their way, assuring them that I seemed harmless. Then she left her desk and took the chair next to me.

"How can I help?" she asked. "I could never believe that Lillian would harm Gary, no matter what."

"You know the family well. I see that. What do you mean by 'no matter what?' "

"I was Gary's assistant for fifteen years. I worked here before old Mr. Brandeis died. The Yarmouths seemed to be an ideal family, always laughing and busy with a thousand activities."

She was avoiding my question, so I moved to another subject. "How did Jack Brandeis get along with Gary and Lillian?"

"Well, to be honest, Gary and Jack didn't see eye to eye when it came to the business. See, Gary was the one with the ideas. He really built on what old Mr. Brandeis had started. He expanded sales. I guess you'd say he was a born salesman. Everyone here loved him. He always had a smile, or a joke to tell. Jack was more the detail man. He likes everything to be organized. Some here say he's a bit stingy, and he thought Gary over-stepped his role in the business and the family."

"Was Jack jealous of Gary?"

"I wouldn't say jealous. But he did resent Gary's relationship with Mr. Brandeis. Before he died, he appointed Gary president of Elite. I guess that hurt Jack."

"Is Jack close to Lillian?"

"Well, he's always been protective of her. She's his kid sister, and Lillian is a quiet woman, devoted to her home and kids. I always thought Gary was good for her. He was so outgoing. If you ever saw Lillian with Gary, it was clear she adored him. I know she'd never hurt him, let alone do what they say she did."

"So what did you mean by Lillian wouldn't hurt him, no matter what?"

"I don't want to cause trouble," Beverly said. "I want to see Lillian get through this." She twisted the lump of Kleenex in her hand.

I reached over and put my hand on hers. "Beverly, if you know something that could hurt Lillian's case, please, tell me. I need to know before the prosecutors dig up some dirt. I can't help if I don't know what I'm fighting."

"Please, don't tell anyone this came from me." She drew a deep breath. "Last year Gary was spending a lot of time on the Omni Hotel account. We supplied most of the hotels in the southeast. Gary said he was trying to get the national account, but he seemed to be having a number of appointments with the local manager,

Maddie Rodriguez. Gary had me setting lunch and dinner reservations. Maddie was calling him here all the time."

Beverly stopped and looked past me. She looked frightened. I turned around and saw a tall, balding man glaring at her.

"Well, you must be Mary Katz," he said. He continued to stare at Beverly, who jumped up and returned to her desk. "I'm sorry. I was detained in the warehouse. The front desk told me you were here waiting."

"I was just keeping her company while she waited," Beverly said.

"Yes, I can see that. Thank you, Beverly. You should have called me."

"I would have, if I'd known where you were," Beverly answered.

"Well, Ms. Katz, let's go into my office. I don't have a lot of time, but I see you are persistent, so let's have our little talk," Jack said.

I followed him down a long hall with pictures of Miami as it had been over the years. We entered a large corner office, well furnished, with the neatest desk I'd ever seen. Beverly was right. This was a man who tended to details.

Jack motioned to the chair across the desk from him. "Now, Ms. Katz, the company and I are prepared to assist Lillian in every way possible. I will tell you straight out that I wanted to hire a more, shall we say, well-known attorney for my sister. I contacted a New York firm. However, Lillian feels that she wants you, so that's that. What is it you want from me?"

"I need to gather all the information possible regarding Gary, his friends, family, his work, anything that will lead to a defense. I'm sure you know that Lillian is in shock and not able to assist me very much at this time."

"Lillian has always been a delicate woman. I did not know that she was unwell. I will call the family doctor."

Jack's expression of impatience was growing. He reminded me of Sam when I'm slow in getting his dog chow served up. I thought he might leap from his chair at any moment.

"I understand that you're very busy, but I need to ask you some questions. Did Gary have any business enemies? Anyone you know of who would have wanted to hurt him?"

"On the contrary, everyone loved Gary. He was Mister Personality."

"Did you share that view?"

"What I thought of him is unimportant. As long as he kept my sister happy, he was okay with me."

"Were you friends as well as family and business colleagues?"

"None of this is really your business, but I'll try to

explain. Gary didn't really fit in to our family or community. He was raised in a very poor family. He lacked many advantages that we grew up with. He expanded his horizons when he married Lillian and came into the business. I'm sure you understand what I mean. Now is there anything else?" Jack started to get up.

"Yes, there is. Was Gary seeing another woman?"

Jack's face turned red. "Why would you ask that?"

"Look, Mr. Brandeis, if Gary was cheating on Lillian, that could be a motive for her having murdered him. The prosecution will use that. I need to know matters like this so I can stop any speculation about a motive. You and I are on the same side. We both want what's best for your sister."

"I know nothing about Gary's personal affairs. Now, if you will excuse me, I must get back to work." Jack was up and opening the door.

"If you remember anything else, please call me at once," I said as I moved out the door. This whole family was a puzzle. Why wouldn't Jack tell me what he knew? And why was it so apparent that he had hated Gary?

CHAPTER TWELVE

My office was just as messy as I had left it. I picked up a bunch of new phone messages on my way in. I realized I'd never had lunch. I found an apple and a candy bar in my desk drawer and washed them down with a cold cup of coffee left over from the morning.

The first phone message was from Ray Abruzzo. His son had been arrested again for car theft. He had posted bond, but needed me to appear at the arraignment. Nothing new there.

The second message caught my attention. Catherine Aynsworth was looking for a paralegal position. One of the secretaries in the building had recommended she call me. I grabbed the phone and dialed the number and extension. She was at German and Duke, a large well-respected firm downtown.

"This is Catherine. May I help you?" a warm voice said.

"Catherine, this is Mary Katz. You called regarding a job. Are you free to talk?"

"I'd like to speak to you in person. I live near your office. May I stop in on my way home this evening?"

"Yes, I'll wait for you." As I hung up, I had a feeling of relief. Maybe my mother was right about the power of prayer. I had been saying, my God, I need help over and over for days. Or maybe it was just that my luck was about to change.

Catherine arrived at five thirty on the dot. She was in her thirties, a single mom supporting two grade-school aged sons. She lived blocks from the office and was avid to get employment close to home.

"I can ride my bike to work. I only have a couple of requests. Sometimes I might need to leave work early to see the kids play soccer," she said. "But I am very organized and I can come back to the office after dinner if necessary."

Her second request was to wear comfortable, non-dressy clothes to work. "I'm on a tight budget. I'm more interested in buying shoes for my kids then ritzy clothes for me." She looked at me expectantly, a pleading in her eyes.

"It's fine with me. Most of our clients are not 'ritzy.' They'll feel more relaxed if you don't look like they can't afford our fees."

She smiled and sat back in her chair for the first time in our interview. We negotiated salary, and agreed on a starting time in one week.

Catherine looked around at my muddled desk and files piled on the floor. "How about I stay here and give you a free hour. Show me to my computer and let's look at the file system," she said.

I wanted to kiss her, but such a move might scare her away. My guardian angel had arrived and her name was Catherine.

It was after seven when I locked up and entered the parking lot, my arms full of files. The first thing I noticed was that my car was the only one left in the lot. It was completely dark out. I had parked in the last space when I returned to the office, out of the range of the safely lights. My SUV appeared to be leaning to one side. I fumbled for my keys and as I opened the hatch door, I realized why the car looked like it was parked on a hill. There are no hills in Miami except for Mt. Trashmore, the toxic landfill.

I had a flat tire, totally without air. "Oh, shit," I yelled into the empty lot.

I called Triple A. Their pat answer was, it'll be at least an hour. You'd think they were dealing with a snow day. My next call to Joe the garage guy who kept my Explorer running, netted only an answer machine. I was doomed to wait for the Triple A guys. I cursed myself for never having learned simple car stuff like changing a tire.

I was about to return to the office when my cell phone rang.

"Hello," I shouted, unable to read the caller ID in the dark lot.

"Mary, where are you?" It was Carlos. "I was a little worried. You didn't answer at home or in the office."

"I'm in the parking lot with a tire as flat as your gorgeous abs."

"I'll be right over."

Fifteen minutes later, the Escalade pulled into the lot. Carlos, still in his construction jeans and boots, jumped out. I threw my arms around him.

"What a great greeting. I think I'll flatten your tires at least once a week," he said.

He pulled a set of tools from the back of the Escalade and began to jack up the car.

"Do you have a spare?" he asked. Then I heard "*Aye caramba.* Mary, look at this."

The tire was off and I saw the slash. Someone had deliberately cut my tire.

"What kind of asshole did this," I screamed.

"Okay, sweetheart, I'm here. I'll get this changed, and then I'll follow you home. Maybe we both need a shower to cool off."

That thought made me forget about the tire for a minute.

CHAPTER THIRTEEN

On Thursday Professor Kominsky and I were climbing the steps of the Dade County Courthouse on our way to an emergency hearing to oppose Frank's restraining order. I had climbed those steps a hundred times with nervous clients in tow. I loved the old building with its pillars, high-ceilinged courtrooms, and historic photos. Miami is a bit short on history, but this building gives the feeling that we've been around a while.

I felt a little unsteady. Karen took my arm and we marched to the elevator.

"You're in luck. We drew Judge Elizabeth Maxwell," said Karen.

"I've met her. She's nice, but why am I lucky."

"She's an advocate for women in the profession. Before she was on the bench, she was the president of the local NOW chapter, and she sits on the board of the National Association of Women Judges. Their main purpose is to foster women in the legal profession. She won't be impressed with a male lawyer trying to keep a female lawyer from earning a living."

Our case was the first one called in the afternoon session. We were seated at the defendant's table. At the plaintiff's table sat Frank surrounded by a phalanx of lawyers; two others from my old firm, one of the old-guard good old boys from a Washington firm with local offices, and a paralegal, unpacking copious papers from their assembled briefcases. Frank was a dunce. He hadn't included one woman in his army of legal talent.

Karen smiled as she approached the lectern. "Good Afternoon, Your Honor. I am —"

"Yes, Professor, of course, I know who you are, and it's good to see you. Let's see, you represent Mary Katz. I've reviewed the pleadings. Mr. Fieldstone is suing Ms. Katz, a former member of his law firm, and wishes the court to enter a temporary restraining order, keeping Ms. Katz from contacting or representing her clients. What seems unusual here is that you, Professor, have requested this emergency hearing. I would have expected Mr. Fieldstone to be the one eager for this hearing."

"Well, Judge, I would have thought so, too, but this is indicative of the game playing that Mr. Fieldstone is engaged in. It appears he is using the court system to get back at Ms. Katz for breaking off their engagement. Of course, Ms. Katz could not remain as a part of Mr. Fieldstone's firm after that. The clients that she has continued to represent are those that she herself brought into the firm."

Fieldstone's lawyers were all on their feet objecting.

"Sit down, gentlemen," the judge said. "You'll have your chance in a few minutes, and when you do, you will select one spokesperson. We're not having double-teaming. Understand? Go ahead, Professor Kominsky."

"Your Honor, I have prepared a chart of all of the clients involved. You will see the date Ms. Katz began representing them, the subject matter of the case, and where the case is in the system. As you can see, most of these cases are criminal matters. No one else at Fieldstone's firm handles criminal cases. Two are being handled pro bono, so if the plaintiff wants to take over that representation as a free contribution, Ms. Katz has no objection. However, Fieldstone generally objected to her handling these matters for free, so it seems unlikely that he will want to do so. May I also approach and hand to you letters from thirty-nine of Ms. Katz's clients expressing their desire to have her continue as their lawyer, and waiving their attorney-client privilege should you wish to hear directly from them."

"This is very impressive. Plaintiff, let's hear your side of this.

The Washington lawyer approached the lectern. "Judge, it's black-letter law. That is, every court in this country frowns on the theft of client files and the outright stealing of client representation. Your Honor will certainly not want to risk being overturned."

"Sir, I've been on the bench for twelve years. I am

confident in my decisions. Every court does not rule in lockstep. The facts vary in every case. Now are you telling me that Mr. Fieldstone has suddenly decided to take up criminal law?"

"Well, I'm not sure, Judge, but . . ."

"I've heard enough. I'm ready to rule. As you all know, the standard for granting a temporary restraining order is whether it appears that the plaintiff's case is so strong that he will prevail at trial. Not only is this case weak, it is crying to be put out of its misery. I will do so now by dismissing this case. Mr. Fieldstone, let me remind you that the court abhors the use of the justice system merely for vindictive purposes. You could end up paying the defendant's attorney fees and court costs. Now, Ms. Katz, you go out there and prosper in your practice. Next case, please."

I thanked Karen a dozen times as we left the courthouse.

"Don't thank me yet. Remember, one down and one still to go. Let's save the celebration until we get rid of the ethics complaint."

I had almost forgotten in my euphoria over outsmarting Franklin Fieldstone, the Harvard lawyer. My next thought was about Lillian's case. How I would love to see her bouncing down the courthouse steps with the same happiness I was feeling. That seemed like a long shot now that I believed another woman had been involved with Gary. Had Lillian heard the rumors? I had to get her family to level with me.

CHAPTER FOURTEEN

The following Monday, Catherine reported for work at eight o'clock. I had a full morning in court followed by an afternoon of depositions. For the first time in weeks, my office was running like a Nascar winner and without my presence. I got messages that actually made sense every time I called in. I returned to the office at five thirty. A stack of neatly typed correspondence was on my desk for signature, all the files were off the floor, and there was a note taped to my computer.

> I hope you don't mind my putting up a few pictures around my desk. Hope everything is satisfactory. See you tomorrow.
>   Catherine
> P.S. I left you some peanut butter cookies that I baked yesterday.

I found the cookies and attacked them. This was as close to heaven as a law office can be. Then I went to look at the pictures. I was anxious to see what Catherine's boys looked like. The pictures were not family type, at least not a human family. There were photographs of wolves in the snow, wolves by a stream, and wolves coming out of a forest. Well, everyone has her own quirks. This one was interesting. There must be a story here. I couldn't wait to hear it.

I got to the office at nine thirty on Tuesday. The luxury of such a late arrival made me feel decadent.

Catherine, who heard me come in the back door, whisked into my office and shut the door. "There's a woman in the waiting room. She doesn't have an appointment. She said it's important that she see you. I rang your house right after she got here. I guessed you were on the way in."

"How long has she been there? What's her name?"

"Oh, sorry, she's Marian Brandeis. She said you'd know who she was. She got here a little before nine. I gave her some coffee. She looks nervous."

"Everyone looks nervous in a lawyer's office. You did good, Catherine. Show her right in." I couldn't imagine why Jack Brandeis's wife was here. Maybe this was a breakthrough, or maybe she was angry about my visit to Jack.

"Right in here, Mrs. Brandeis," Catherine said.

Marian Brandeis was probably in her mid-fifties. She wore a designer knit pantsuit and expensive pumps. Her short dark hair was cut to precision, revealing gorgeous diamond earrings. She was slightly plump. She must have been a beautiful young girl, and was still a handsome woman.

She stared at me and around the office, her eyes darting in nervous flickers, as she perched on the end of the seat across from me.

"Ms. Katz, I'm sorry to barge in on you like this, but I just had to talk to you," she said.

"That's perfectly all right, and please, call me Mary. Let's move over to the sofa. You'll be more comfortable. Now what can I do for you."

"I know you're doing your best to represent Lillian. Jack told me about your visit with him. First, I want to apologize for his attitude."

"It's okay. I know it's hard to talk to a complete stranger about family matters."

"I know the reason he's reluctant to talk to you. Someone's got to tell you why. You need to know what Jack and I know about Gary, even if it hurts Lillian's case."

"Just a minute, Mrs. Brandeis," I said. I buzzed Catherine and told her to hold any calls, and be sure there were no interruptions. I closed the door and locked it.

"Do you mind if I take some notes?" I asked as I reached for my yellow legal pad.

"You can call me Marian, please, and please don't tell Jack that I came to see you."

"Okay. Just take your time, and tell me all you can about Lillian and Gary. Remember, nothing surprises me. Lawyers hear confidential information all the time as part of their job."

"I never really trusted Gary. I know Lillian adored

him, but all that patting people on the back and taking your hand and not letting go, it was creepy."

"Did Jack distrust him too?"

"Of course. The way he wormed his way into his dad's good graces. It was nauseating. Then I really found out about him."

"Please, tell me what you found out."

Marian looked around as if an eavesdropper were about to come out of the woodwork. She sighed and reached in her purse. I thought she was about to hand me some evidence, but she retrieved a cigarette and a gold lighter. I have a big "please do not smoke" sign on my desk, but I was afraid she would spook and end our tell-all session.

"Well, I was in New York in the fall. I went with the Miami City Ballet. The whole board went for their performance at Lincoln Center; moral support, you know. Well, thank goodness, I was shopping by myself when it happened," Marian said.

"Go ahead," I said.

"I was coming out of Barney's when I saw them."

"Who?" My patience was wearing thin.

"Gary and that woman. They were holding hands. Just strolling along Madison Avenue, like no one would see them."

"Who was the woman?"

"I later found out who she was. Maddie Rodriguez. She looked young enough to be his daughter. She was carrying a big Saks shopping bag, and looking at Gary and giggling. I just stood there and stared. They didn't even notice me. Too absorbed in each other. So I decided to follow them. They turned up Central Park South and went into the Park Lane Hotel."

"Did you tell anyone else about this? Like Lillian?"

"I'd never tell Lillian, but I rushed back to my hotel and called Jack. I was so upset. I don't know how I got through the rest of that trip."

"What did Jack say? Did he tell Lillian?"

"As far as I know, no one told Lillian. At least I don't think so, because she didn't seem to have any problems. She was planning a trip to Scotland for golf for the two of them and they went two weeks later. Jack said he was going to take care of everything. He was going to confront Gary."

"Did he do that?"

"When they got back from Scotland, they went up to Dartmouth for parents weekend, and then it was Thanksgiving and Christmas and their kids were home, and our kids and grandkids were here, and then there was a strike in France and the French shipments didn't get in, so everyone was rushing around trying to fill orders at the business. But right after New Year's, Jack came home one night and said he found out the redheaded bitch was actually a client from one of the hotels, and that he had had a sit-down with Gary."

"Did Gary admit anything?"

"Well, sort of. He told Jack he was sorry. Jack told him to end this affair now or he would have to tell

Lillian. He also told Gary he should think about stepping down as president of the company, that Dad
Brandeis would be turning over in his grave."

"Marian, that sounds like blackmail. Give up the
company or Jack would tell Lillian. Did Gary stop seeing Maddie?"

"Gary told Jack he would break it off. But I don't
think he did. We were at their house a few weeks ago.
Our cousins were in town. Gary got a phone call. He
left the table. When he came back, he looked upset.
He looked guilty, if you ask me."

"I need to ask you a tough question," I said. "Do
you think Lillian knew, and if she did, would she have
gone a bit crazy and tried to hurt Gary?"

"I can't picture her hurting anyone. She couldn't
even stand it when their dog got hurt. I had to help
her get him to the vet."

"I'm glad you told me, Marian. I know it wasn't
easy for you to come here. Now I know what I need to
investigate. You did the right thing."

"Please, don't tell Jack that I told you. He's such a
private person and so protective of his family."

"I understand. I'll keep this meeting just between
us."

I walked her to the front of the building and
waved as she drove off. So Jack had blackmailed Gary.
I needed to know a lot more about Jack.

CHAPTER FIFTEEN

My morning schedule was already shot when Catherine buzzed me. "There's a man here who says he's Carlos's cousin."

"What's his name, and what does he want?"

"He says his name is Franco, and he's here to do something with your car. He's in the parking lot."

I called Carlos on his cell phones. Neither answered, so I tried the satellite phone in his car. He answered that one on the second ring.

"Who is your cousin Franco, and what does he want with my car?" I asked.

"Oh, I forgot to tell you. I sent Franco over to put a new tire on your SUV. He takes care of all the cars in the family."

"You didn't have to do that. Is he really your cousin?"

"Well, not exactly. He's my brother's wife's cousin. I told him to go over your car while he's there. Make sure that no one has done anything else to it besides the tire. And don't try to pay him. It'll hurt his feelings. Just give him the keys, and he'll do his thing."

I went out to the parking lot where a skinny kid was leaning against a truck that said Franco's Auto Service. I guessed this must be Franco.

"Hi, Franco, I'm Mary. Here are my keys. It's the red Explorer by the door. Thanks for coming over."

"Are you kidding? It's my pleasure. I'd do anything for Carlos. He said you were a great looking chick. He wasn't exaggerating. Say, while I'm here, do you handle divorces?"

"Why, do you want one?"

"I'm thinking about it. My old lady's getting on my nerves. I'll let you know."

He strode over to my car, opened the hood, and began taking things apart. I went back inside and prayed the car would start later.

Back in my office again, I reread the notes I had made during Marian's visit. I hadn't even finished the first page when Catherine approached my desk.

"There's a lady in the waiting room who says she's your mother. She looks just like you, only older, so I guess she really is your mother."

I couldn't believe it. I had put off telling Mother that I was in a new office, in a new relationship, and without Frank's two-karat engagement ring. I ran a comb through my hair, and raced into the waiting room. It was Mother all right and she looked furious.

"Come on back and see my new space," I said as I hugged her.

She didn't return the hug and followed me into the office. I closed the door. Mother never raises her voice. She knows how to snarl without screaming.

"When were you going to tell me that you left Frank's firm? I had to find out from the receptionist when I called there and they said they didn't know how to reach you. I called Jonathan. It seems both your brothers knew all about your complete change of work and boyfriends, but you couldn't bother telling me."

The phone rang and Catherine suppressed a laugh. "Now your father is on the phone. He doesn't sound too happy."

My father does know how to yell, and he was proving that point as Catherine put him through.

"Mary, this is your father. Is your mother there? How could you upset her like that? She drove out of here like a maniac. Did she get there?"

"Yes, Dad, she's here. Why didn't you drive her, if you were so worried?"

"You know I can't miss the men's morning golf at the club."

My parents sold the family house on Miami Beach when Dad sold the Katz Kosher Foods business. They shocked the whole family by moving to a gated development in Boynton Beach, two counties away. Dad's new occupation since retirement is golf. My brothers and I know if there is a family emergency, it must take place in the evenings when the golf course is closed.

"Mary, what are you trying to do? Break your mother's heart? You couldn't tell her that you broke up with Frank?"

I was holding the phone away from my ear to protect my eardrum. Mother grabbed the receiver.

"Abe, stop screaming. I'm okay. I'll handle this." She hung up the phone.

"Listen, Mother, I'm very sorry," I said. "Everything happened so fast. Frank just wasn't the person for me. I met Carlos and I realized Frank was a mistake. Carlos helped me get this great office, and then I had to get all my clients moved to my new practice, and I've got that big murder case that you saw in the paper, and then Frank sued me, but that case has been dismissed —well, you can see I haven't had a minute."

"Carlos? Carlos who?"

"He's my new boyfriend. I'm sorry you're disappointed about Franklin."

"You're wrong. I'm not disappointed about Franklin. I never liked him. He's so stuffy. When can we meet Carlos?"

"Soon, I guess." I was stupefied. "You didn't like Frank, and you never said anything?"

"All I want for you is to see you settled down with a nice home and children. Your clock is ticking. Before you know it, your reproductive years will just be a memory.

"Now let me buy you a nice lunch and you can tell me all about Carlos. And why don't you do something about your hair?"

The morning was gone. I hadn't caught up on any work. I grabbed my purse and followed Mother out the door like a good little girl.

CHAPTER SIXTEEN

The next day was Lillian's official arraignment. I had prepared several motions, as well. I called the condo, and was pleasantly surprised to hear Lillian answer. I reminded her that we needed to be in court promptly at nine o'clock. Her community control officer had also phoned to remind her.

"I'm doing better, Mary. The doctor has me on some tranquilizers. It'll be good to get out of these four walls even though it's a trip to court. The officer said she'd meet us there."

"Shall I pick you up?"

"No, Sherry and Brett will be coming with me."

"I have to prepare you. The media will be covering this. There will be reporters and TV cameras outside. The judge may keep them out of the courtroom, but you'll still have to pass through them at the entrance. It will be easier if I pick you up. I can drive you into the underground garage and you can take an elevator up from there and avoid the reporters."

"Okay, Mary, we'll be waiting in front of our building whenever you say."

The morning was one of the reasons snowbirds flock to Miami in winter. The sun rose early and by the time I picked up the Yarmouth clan, there was a rosy glow over Miami Beach. The sky and the water meshed into a turquoise blanket. Even the causeway traffic seemed subdued.

The contrast between Miami Beach and the Civic Center was never more evident. Cars crawled past the criminal courthouse searching out parking. Two large vans from the outlying jails were trying to plow through the traffic, their windows blacked out and barred as if they contained zoo animals. Nervous families dashed across the street in front of the courthouse, ignoring the cars and vans, concentrating on arriving in the correct courtroom to support their defendant relatives.

"I'm glad you picked us up," Sherry said. "I didn't know this would be such a scene."

Lillian and Brett had remained quiet for the entire ride. Lillian was dressed in a dark suit that made her look paler than ususal. Dark circles rimmed her eyes. No amount of makeup could hide them. I kept my fingers crossed that she could get through the hearing without falling apart like a rootless tree in a windstorm.

We pulled into the garage under the courthouse. It was really the first floor of the building. Those entering through the front doors had to march up thirty steps. The guard in the booth approached my window.

"José, it's me, Mary. How've you been? Listen, I've got Lillian Yarmouth here, you know the big case in courtroom 6-1 today. I need to keep the media circus from trapping her."

"*Oye*, Mary. You know I'd like to help you, but I'm not supposed to let anyone in here who doesn't have a parking sticker. I could get in trouble, maybe lose my job."

"José, you could never lose your job. You've been here through three different state attorneys. The place can't run without you. I'll square everything with the court. You know I'd never hang you out to dry."

I extended my hand through the window and did the ten-dollar handshake. José pocketed the bill, raised the gate and pointed to a parking place near the freight elevator.

We boarded the creaky freight elevator. I pushed six and kept my finger on the number, hoping to bypass the other floors. We stopped anyway on the first floor, the doors opened, and the noise level exploded over us. I pushed "door close." We made it to the sixth floor. Most of the crowd of curiosity seekers and media vultures were already in the courtroom holding down prime-time seating.

Lillian's case had been moved to the ceremonial courtroom to accommodate the crowd. Metal detectors blocked the entrance.

"I thought all the security was at the front doors." Brett finally had something to say. "That's where they were when we came for the bond hearing."

"They're still there. These are a second set that they use whenever there's a high-profile case," I said. I was surprised that this case warranted the extra security, usually reserved for high-level drug dealers or racially inflaming cases.

Lillian and I took our seats at the defense table. Sherry and Brett were seated in the front row right behind us, after I asked "Moe and Curly" to move. Moe and Curly are two of the courthouse regulars. No one is sure of their real names. They attend trials almost every day, using the courts as their regular entertainment. Both appear to be in their eighties. Moe walks with a cane, and Curly is totally bald. They have their favorite lawyers to cheer on. I have been on their list ever since I won a case in which my clients, a retired couple, were accused of running a boiler-room operation selling water purifiers. Moe and Curly admire entrepreneurial skills in fellow retirees.

Karl Morris was seated at the prosecutors' table flanked by two young lawyers. All three got up and started toward our table. I stood up and extended my hand as they approached.

"Good, morning, Mary. This is Charlene Montavo and Charlie Goldberg. They'll be assisting me in this case. Lois McIver will be here from the appellate staff at a later time," Karl said.

I shook hands with each of them. It reminded me of the coin toss before a football game. The big difference was that their team was a lot larger than ours. The bailiff interrupted our ritual.

"All rise. Court is now in session in and for Miami-Dade County. Judge Harvey Arnold presiding. Turn off all pagers and cell phones or they *will* be confiscated. Be seated."

I drew in my breath. "Is everything okay, Mary?" Lillian tugged on my sleeve.

"Just fine. Sit down. Here's a pad and pen. If you need to tell me anything, just write it on the pad, so no one else can hear you," I said.

Things weren't just fine. Harvey Arnold was a recent addition to the bench. He was an unknown quantity. In his past life he had been a commercial litigator. He had little or no knowledge of criminal law. Why had he been assigned to this case? I never bought that blind filing system by the clerk's office. It was as blind as a sharpshooter.

Rumor had it that this circuit court judgeship was just a stepping-stone for Harvey. He hankered after a seat on the appellate court, but without criminal experience he wouldn't be considered, so Lillian's case was going to be his training ground.

"The first case this morning on the arraignment calendar is *State vs. Lillian Yarmouth*," Judge Arnold announced.

Lillian and I approached one lectern, while Karl

stood behind the other. The arraignment is the first time formal charges are filed in court. The state had been holding the indictment in secret. All of my phone calls to Karl had been stonewalled. The clerk's office claimed that they had not received a copy of the charges. The entire courtroom appeared to be holding its collective breath awaiting the degree of the charges. I was hoping for a manslaughter charge, assuming the State would look at the crime as one of passion, a spur-of-the-moment decision by whoever was the killer.

"Good morning, Your Honor," Karl said. The state is filing a one-count indictment against Mrs. Yarmouth for the second degree murder of her spouse, Gary Yarmouth."

A gasp resounded from the audience. Lillian swayed slightly and grabbed my arm. I heard a sob behind me and knew it was Sherry.

"However, Your Honor, I think it advisable to warn the defendant and her counsel that this charge may be superseded by an indictment for first degree murder. We have reason to believe that there was premeditation. The state attorney's death penalty committee is scheduled to meet in March to evaluate whether we will be seeking the death penalty." Karl finished with a flourish.

"How say you, Ms. Katz, on behalf of your client?" the judge inquired.

I was as dizzy as if I had just gotten off a roller

coaster ride. "We enter a plea of not guilty, waive reading of the indictment, request immediate discovery, fifteen days for further motions, and request a very early trial date." My lawyer mind had returned. I would ram this case to a swift conclusion before these gestapo prosecutors dreamed up any other tortures for Lillian. "Also, Judge, you will notice that I have filed other motions to be heard this morning."

"Judge, I was unaware of any motions calendared for today," Karl whined.

"These motions were delivered one week ago to the state. The court file will reflect the date they were served." I smiled at the clerk who was already going through the court file.

"She's right, Your Honor," the clerk said, as she passed the papers to the judge. "Date of service was actually nine days ago."

One of the young assistants was rushing forward with the motions from Karl's file. Karl gave her a dirty look and began to study the documents.

"My first motion is to remove Mrs. Yarmouth from the electronic monitor. She has posted a one-million-dollar bond with her family home as collateral. She has lived her whole life in Miami. Her children have left college to live with her while this case is pending. Her brother and sister-in-law live nearby and the family business is located here as well. All of these safeguards insure that my client will never leave the county."

"What are you asking me to do?" Harvey asked.

"Judge, you can't be considering this." Karl's voice rose in a grating squeak. "I was going to ask you to revoke her bond and put her in jail."

Lillian began to cry. I patted her shoulder.

"I believe the bond itself is sufficient without any further impediments. I need my client to assist in her defense. That means she needs to be free to come to my office and to attend the depositions of State witnesses. If you feel that you need some other protective measures, how about having her report to a community control officer twice a week?" I asked.

The judge scratched his head, looking around the courtroom for help. He looked at Lillian for a long minute. Then he spoke in a soft voice. "Mrs. Yarmouth, I think I can trust that you will show up in court for all hearings. You've posted a large bond. If you fail to appear, the courts and/or the bondsman would own your home. That is safeguard enough. I will remove the electronic monitor. You will report to an officer every Monday morning at nine a.m."

"Oh, thank you, Your Honor. You won't be sorry," Lillian said, and for the first time since I met her, she smiled.

"I can't believe it," Karl muttered as he left the lectern.

"I beg your pardon. Would you like to repeat that, so everyone can hear, including the court reporter in case she missed that," the judge said.

"I have a few more matters to address, Your

Honor," I said, "if the state would return to the lectern."

"Maybe you should quit while you're ahead," the judge said. He was beginning to enjoy himself. He relaxed and leaned back in his chair.

"I don't have the luxury of quitting, Judge. My client is charged with a heinous crime of which she is not guilty. There is not one iota — not one scintilla — of evidence that she is the perpetrator."

"Your Honor," Karl interrupted, "she's making a speech for the press."

"I resent that, Judge. I am sworn to be an advocate for my client. That's what I am doing."

Of course I was hoping the press had picked up on my remarks, but if not, there was always the press conference after court.

"I have asked for immediate discovery, and I note that none has been given. I plan to take depositions as soon as I can serve the state's witnesses. I am especially eager to get the tape of the nine-one-one call to the Miami Police, where we will hear Mrs. Yarmouth's voice. She reported finding her husband's body. I am asking the court to instruct the police department not to destroy that tape."

"So ordered," said Judge Arnold. "State, why didn't you turn over your witness list and other discovery this morning when you filed the indictment? Isn't that how it's usually done?"

"Well, Judge, we're working on it. It should be

ready in about ten days," Karl said. He was looking down at his shoes.

"Then, if I can't have discovery right away, I am asking the court for a preliminary hearing. I know this is rarely done under our state system. That's because we have full discovery in criminal cases including depositions, but the prosecution is trying to stonewall my ability to view their evidence. A preliminary hearing will show the court that there is no evidence against Lillian, I mean Mrs. Yarmouth." I paused for breath. "And I am asking for a trial date in ninety days."

"Ninety days?" Karl yelled. "This is a murder case. Ms. Katz knows it takes at least a year to bring a murder case to trial, sometimes two, and I have other older serious cases."

"That's your problem, Mr. Morris. It's very refreshing to hear a lawyer ask for a quick trial date. All I've heard since I began my judgeship is 'continuance, continuance.'"

"Ms. Katz, I think a preliminary hearing just might be a good idea. Two weeks from today, one p.m. Next case, please."

I led Lillian out of the courtroom. I really felt like skipping out of the courtroom, but I contained myself. It wasn't so bad having a judge who didn't know shit about criminal court. He was making it up as he went, and I was helping. Now we were ready to talk to the press. The cameras were clicking as we left the courtroom.

CHAPTER SEVENTEEN

The weekend loomed ahead. I was behind in all my work, and had planned to spend most of it in the office until Carlos reminded me that I had agreed to spend it with his parents on Marco Island at their beach condo.

"Can we compromise? Please?" I asked.

"Don't tell me you're backing out of meeting my family," Carlos said.

"Of course not. I'm looking forward to it," I said. I just need to work. Can't we go for the day on Saturday and come back Saturday night? Then I can work all day Sunday." I tried not to blink as Carlos stared at me.

It was only a partial lie. I did have to work. I wasn't looking forward to being examined by Carlos's parents.

"Okay, but bring your bathing suit. I hope it's a bikini. And bring a change for dinner. My mother has asked a few other guests."

So it wasn't just a once-over by the parents. A whole firing squad of Latino critics was going to pass judgment as well. I called my hairdresser for an emergency hair cut and pedicure.

Saturday dawned darkly. The sun was covered by banks of clouds. It rarely rains in February or early March. In fact, this is the season when wildfires begin due to the months of dry weather. The weatherman on Channel 7 was ecstatic. "It looks like rain is coming in from the west and we need it badly," he crooned.

I needed rain like I needed an extra hole in my head. What would we do all day if we couldn't hang out at the beach?

The ride across Alligator Alley, the old name for I-75, used to be one of my favorites, right through the Everglades. When we were kids and the road had been a two-laner, my brothers and I spent the ride with noses pressed to the windows looking for who could spot an alligator or an eagle. Now it was a freeway. But birds still filled the area. I concentrated on counting the species. The sky grew darker and soon rain splashed against the windshield in big ugly drops.

We turned off the freeway and onto the island, passing hotels, motels, restaurants, and condos. Carlos turned down a small road almost hidden in the foliage. We traveled another mile and pulled in front of a group of townhouses. Behind the buildings we could hear the waves of the gulf against the seawall. Carlos grabbed my canvas bag and walked me around the houses to a stunning, peaceful beach. I took a big whiff of the sea air.

"I told you this was a great place," Carlos said. "This is where I come to chill out."

The door opened at the top of a winding stairway leading up from the beach. An attractive woman dressed in a designer-type warm-up suit called out.

"Carlos, don't just stand there. I've been waiting."

"We're coming, *Mamacita*. Just showing Mary the beach."

We moved out of the rain and the spray of the waves. As we approached, I saw that Angelina Martin was a tiny woman, but this hadn't hindered her ability to be adorned in a diamond necklace and bracelet and large gold earrings. She threw her arms around me, stabbing me with the diamonds, and kissing me on each cheek. I wasn't sure how to respond, so I gave a light hug in return.

"Come in, come in. I have breakfast all ready for you. It's really brunch. J.C. come out here."

A tall handsome man appeared. He looked a lot like Carlos, except for his mustache and salt-and-pepper hair. He had the same amazing smile.

As we walked into the dining room, I looked at the view of the beach through the sliding glass doors. Carlos and his dad hugged and smiled at each other, and the sun came out.

The day passed pleasantly. We had rum drinks on the beach and a ride in J.C.'s fishing boat, which was larger than some people's apartments. I learned that J.C. stood for Juan Carlos. I learned that several cousins would be joining us for dinner at the beach club.

After we dressed for dinner, I had my opportunity to ask Angelina about her position on the board of directors at Elite Wines.

"I don't mean to sound nosy. You know that I represent Lillian Yarmouth. I'm trying to find out everything I can that will help me defend her," I said.

"Carlos tells me that you're a very smart lawyer. I'm sure you'll represent her well. Of course, in my day women left such work to the men. We were busy raising children and making our homes run smoothly. Lots of Hispanic women still find that very fulfilling," Angelina said.

"A number of Hispanic women who I went to law school with are practicing law or running businesses in Miami. That's the nice part of being female. There's something that suits everyone. Don't you think?" I said. I smiled, trying to conceal my annoyance.

"I suppose. What is it that you want to know about Elite? I really don't know all that much about those people. I know they asked me on to the board because J.C. has connections to retail wine merchants in the Hispanic community, and he has connections to some of the South American wineries. This is a Chilean wine that you are drinking now. Isn't it delicious?"

"Yes, it's very nice. What did you think of Gary Yarmouth? You must have observed him at board meetings."

"Oh, sure. He was the kind of guy that you either

loved him or you hated him. Lillian adored him. She hung on every word out of his mouth."

"Who hated him?"

"Marian Brandeis, Jack's wife. She was on the board too. I think she resented him. She mostly voted 'no' for anything he suggested. She always lost."

"What did you think of Gary?"

"He was a real charmer, a lady's man. Always complimenting me on my clothes or jewelry. Always putting an arm around the women, even the secretaries. It was a bit much, but it didn't bother me. It didn't even seem to bother Lillian at all. I would have been livid if he were my *esposo*. Jack always looked a little annoyed. Jack's a solid guy. He'll be good for Elite. I assume he'll be taking the presidency at the next board meeting. There isn't anyone else."

"There's Lillian. She must own a large part of the company."

"That's ridiculous. She's not a business person, and besides she's accused of murder right now."

Carlos and his father came in, and the conversation stopped. It was time to go to dinner, and time for me to face the Martin family review board. I gulped the rest of my wine hoping to withstand the inspection.

Dinner was a noisy and festive affair. The various cousins were actually a collection of distant relatives and closer friends. For instance, Marielena was the cousin of Angelina's sister-in-law, but everyone called her Auntie. Walter was an old friend of J.C.'s uncle in Argentina and spent part of his time helping Carlos's younger brother who ran the cattle ranch in Argentina that had belonged to Carlos's grandfather. I was going to need a chart to keep everyone straight. I concentrated on just remembering their names for the evening.

I was enjoying the gregariousness of this group, and found myself getting into the kidding and jokes. Then Marielena moved over next to me during dessert. Carlos had gotten up to procure another bottle of wine. Marielena slipped into his empty seat.

"Did you actually meet Carlos at a car wash or was that just Carlos kidding us?" she asked.

"No, no joke. We met at a car wash, after he rear-ended my car," I said.

"So it was like he picked you up. Is that the expression?"

"It wasn't at all like that. Actually, I ended up representing him in a legal matter." I tried to hide my irritation the way you try to hide a spot on your shirt. I covered my face for a moment.

"Carlos told his mother he was going to marry you."

"Maybe that was a little premature. We haven't known each other very long."

"You know, Mary, sometimes it's hard for Anglo

girls to fit into Spanish families. I hope you won't take offense. Carlos has already gone through one divorce. I just want to see him happily settled."

Now I was angry and I didn't care if it showed. Marielena was a busybody, and a prejudiced one. "If I remember correctly, Carlos's original wife was Hispanic, so I guess marriages fail for reasons beyond ethnicity. That's correct, isn't it?" I said in my best cross-examination voice.

Carlos appeared, carrying a bottle of sparkling wine. His presence ended round one in the Anglo-Hispanic slap down. Marielena got up, gave Carlos a peck on the cheek, and returned to her seat next to Angelina. I watched as she whispered in Angelina's ear. They acted like two little girls in study hall, talking trash about the teacher.

I reminded Carlos that I needed to get home to be fresh for work in the morning. We gave our regrets for the early departure. It looked like the party was just warming up. This would give everyone time to discuss the Gringo girl who was trying to steal Carlos.

CHAPTER EIGHTEEN

I woke up Sunday feeling slightly hungover. Between the rum and the wine, it was a miracle that I was able to get up. I wanted to get to the office, but my head was buzzing. I made a strong pot of coffee and drank it all. Sam gulped down his breakfast, and demanded a walk.

The walk did not clear my head. I decided to put off the office for a while. An hour at the gym might restore my equilibrium. I hoped Carlos wouldn't call at the office. I had resisted his staying over, pleading I really needed sleep, and a full day of catch-up work.

The gym was one of a chain of health clubs. It was large, well lighted, and always crowded from six a.m. until midnight. The noise of the machines, the weights hitting the floor, and the pounding feet on the dozens of treadmills was not a good cure for the hangover. The good thing about the early-morning crowd was that it was made up of serious gym rats. They were there for exercise, not ogling or conversing.

I decided on the stationary bike, because it didn't

make any noise. I grabbed the front of the *Miami Herald* and began to pedal away. Twenty minutes later, I was sweaty but sane again. I moved to the health juice bar, and sat down on the only empty stool. I looked to my right and saw a familiar looking young guy. For a minute, I couldn't place him, and then it hit me.

"Brett Yarmouth. How are you?"

"Oh, hi, Mary. I was just leaving," he said. He leapt from the stool as if I had bitten him.

"Wait," I said and grabbed his arm. "I really need to talk to you. Why haven't you come to the office to meet with me?"

"What's the point? You've met with Sherry. I don't know what I could add."

"You never know. The event you think is unimportant could be the very thing that will help your mother. Look, we're both here. We can go out on the patio and talk informally. You may have to be a witness for your mother, so sooner or later I have to talk with you. You know, to prepare you to testify. Come on, you want to help your mother, don't you?"

"Of course, it's just that—"

"I'm not taking no for answer." I took Brett by the elbow, grabbed my health-bar smoothie, and steered him to the door. What could he be hiding that was feeding his reluctance to speak to me, or was he reluctant to help his mother?

The patio was deserted except for an attendant putting towels out for the water aerobics class at eleven.

With any luck, we would have a quiet hour out here.

"Have you decided when you'll go back to school?" I asked

"If I miss another month, it'll be too late for this term. I was going to have to go this summer anyway and so was Sherry, so we'll plan on the summer quarter, if everything's okay here, of course."

"What's your major?"

"That's a good question. Damned if I know. Dad wanted me to go into the business. Dartmouth has a good MBA program, and I thought I'd get a master's and then work at Elite. At least, that's what I thought when I finished high school, but things change."

"I'm sure it's hard to think about your family's business now with your dad gone, but your mother still owns part of Elite."

"I made my decision not to be in business with my dad and Uncle Jack way before this mess. Too many family squabbles, and other stuff."

"What other stuff?"

"Just family stuff."

"Listen, Brett, I don't know what you're hiding. I'm not your enemy. If you know something that's going to come out at trial, please don't leave me in the dark. You can help me do my job."

Brett looked out at the pool. He shifted in his seat and finally turned and looked at me. For a minute, I thought he was going to cry. He swallowed hard. His hands were balled into fists in his lap. He looked like a kid who needed a parent. I'm not the maternal type, but I needed to seize the moment, so I moved over next to Brett and put an arm around him.

"The longer you carry around a secret, the worse it may seem in your mind. Maybe you'll feel better if you share whatever is bothering you. We'll sort it out together," I said.

"I'm scared that what I tell you may hurt my mother's case. Like maybe you'll think she did it."

"I can assure you that even if I had doubts about her innocence, it wouldn't affect my duty to represent her to the fullest. I'm a good judge of character, and I have no doubts about her. I think the police made a huge mistake and jumped to the conclusion that she committed this murder. They never really investigated. Just said case closed, and gave themselves a gold star."

Brett took a deep breath and spoke almost in a whisper. "Last summer I came home between quarters for a couple of weeks. You know Dartmouth is pretty much of a year-round school. I planned to spend the time interning at the office, learning the products. In the fall, I was going to spend a few weeks in France interning at one of the wineries." Brett cleared his throat and paused.

"Take your time, I said. "I've got all day free."

"I went to Dad's office to see if he wanted to go to lunch. I didn't knock. I never do. I mean he was my dad. I opened the door and caught him with some slut. I mean she had her blouse off and he was sucking her tits. I couldn't believe it. I mean right in his office, like he didn't care who saw him. I was furious. I walked out and slammed the door."

"He chased after me. He could see I was shocked or pissed or whatever. He insisted that we leave and go talk over lunch. I said what if Mom had walked in there, or Uncle Jack or Beverly. He said he was sorry, and begged me not to tell Mom or Sherry. He said the woman didn't mean anything to him and that he had been weak. That she had been coming on to him."

"Did you find out who she was?"

"Not then. I made him promise that he wouldn't see her anymore or I would tell Mom. He promised, and I believed him."

"So was that the end of it?" I asked. I knew it wasn't. Marian had seen Gary and Maddie in New York in the fall.

"I really wanted to believe him for Mom's sake. In the fall, Dad was going to New York on business. I called him at his hotel. I had this great idea that I'd come down to New York, and we'd go to a Mets game. They were playing our team, the Marlins. Dad always loved taking me to ball games, and I wanted to see him before I left for France. He sounded real strange. Said he had too many plans with clients and he'd have to take a rain check. I had a bad feeling that he was lying."

"No one likes to find out that their parents aren't perfect. You just found it out later than a lot of kids," I said.

"I still never said anything to anybody. Then we came home for Christmas. Mom seemed fine, but Dad was moody and quiet. He kept getting phone calls and going into his office to talk. I knew he was still seeing that slut, so I walked in while he was on one of the calls. He hung up, and I told him straight out that I had to tell Mom. He was being unfair, and he broke his promise to me.

I never saw my dad fall apart before. He was always the happy guy who we all leaned on. He sat down and just lost it. He told me he'd made an awful mistake, playing around with a client from one of the hotel chains. I guess he thought he'd have a little fun and that would be it. Maybe he'd done this before."

"Was her name Maddie Rodriguez?" I asked.

"So you already knew about this?" Brett jumped up. His face turned red.

My big mouth ruined the rapport I had just established.

"I did a little digging and that name came up. I didn't know how she was connected to your dad," I lied. "Please, I didn't mean to interrupt you. I hope you'll tell me what else you know about this, so that I can understand what was occurring in your family,"

Brett sat down. "Dad said she wouldn't leave him alone. She wanted him to buy her a condo. She was threatening him. He said he never meant for something like this to go this far, and he would find a way to end it for good. He said Mom didn't know and he begged me not to tell her. So I went back to school after New Year's. I was upset about this whole thing, which was why I decided to get home for Presidents' Day weekend to see how everything was. Sherry decided to come with me."

"Did you tell her about this?"

"I haven't told anyone except my roommate, and now, you."

"I'm not sure that I understand why you were so reluctant to tell me." I could have been unprepared for the State in court."

"You mean they know?"

"If they don't know now, they will before this case is over. It's their job to establish a motive, a reason why someone would commit a murder."

"See, that's what I thought. If people knew how my dad had cheated on my mom, they'd believe that she did kill him. I felt like killing him myself. And sometimes I wonder if she found out and, well, maybe she did do it. Maybe she caught him like I did."

"Has your mother ever done anything violent that you can remember?"

"Never. She never even spanked us. She hates violence. Won't even watch a movie with killing."

"Okay, Brett, you did the right thing telling me all of this. I need to find out more about this woman. One more question. How did your Uncle Jack and your father get along?"

"They argued a lot about the business. They

weren't close, but Jack's an okay guy. He knew how much Mom cared for Dad, so he tried to keep his feelings to himself."

"Are you all right, Brett? Should I drive you home?"

"No, I've got a car here. I think I'll go for a swim before I go back home."

"Don't be afraid to come and talk to me anytime," I said. I gave him a kiss on the cheek. He waved as I walked back through the gym.

I went right to the office, sweaty workout clothes or not. This was the time to lay out everything I knew about Lillian's case. I put down everything I had learned from Brett, and began comparing it to my other notes.

Some mail had arrived on Saturday, which I picked up in the front hall mail slot. Now I glanced at the top envelope. It contained the first discovery documents from the state attorney's office. There were three attached sheets containing the police arrest report. It was in the usual police condition, written by the first officers on the scene in a scrawling handwriting, hard to decipher. I was sure by now the homicide officers had written a full typewritten offense incident report. The State was doling out the discovery in slow motion. The last time I was involved in a case with the Miami P.D., they claimed that all reports had to be approved by a captain before being disbursed to the defense. The captain must have needed remedial reading because I had waited over a month for that report. I was not going to let them stall this time. I read the messy handwriting with difficulty.

Arrived at the Bayshore Road residence of Yarmouth family at 3:17 p.m. Dispatched re: 911 of a 28 at residence. Reporter Lillian Yarmouth. Fire Rescue on scene at 3:21. Victim, Gary Yarmouth, age 49, located in upstairs bedroom, stab wound to heart. DOA. Weapon still in body, silver paper knife with monogram LLB. Fire rescue removed weapon, given to Ofer. Moreno who placed in evidence. No one on scene other than spouse, Lillian Yarmouth. No statement made. Only repeated, "I loved him." House search, no one else in house. No evidence of forced entry. House neat and orderly except for bedroom where signs of a struggle. Desk chair overturned.

Homicide arrived at 4:14, lead detective Harry Fonseca. This officer sent to canvas neighborhood. Interviewed neighbor Cassie Kahn, next door. Witness states she was in her yard

and observed Lillian Yarmouth drive
into garage around 3 p.m. Also saw unknown blonde or red-haired woman run
down Bayshore and enter a vehicle, red
BMW, no license tag given, in vicinity
of home of Hernandez residence two
doors from victim's residence No answer
at Hernandez residence.

Elderly neighbor at 2028
Bayshore, west of victim saw or heard
nothing.

No other neighbors at home.

Medical Examiner's office on scene
at 4:40. Body removed for autopsy.
Crime scene secured and turned over to
homicide who arrested Lillian
Yarmouth at 4:48 p.m. This officer
cleared scene at 4:56 after search of
curtilage and grassy swale areas. Officer
Raul Gordon, Badge #286.

I read the report again. Now I had some witnesses to talk to. I stood up from my desk and stretched just as a crash sounded behind me. I turned to see shards of glass on my desk and chair.

CHAPTER NINETEEN

A rock lay on the floor just under the window behind my desk. My God, if I hadn't stood up, I'd probably be unconscious or brain dead. I began to shake. Was this just some kids out for a Sunday prank or was I actually a target of someone? First my tire, now this.

Without even thinking, I grabbed my cell phone and hit speed dial. Carlos answered the first cell number I hit. Thank goodness I had his numbers on speed dial. My hands were too shaky to punch out numbers or even remember them.

"Hey, thought you were working. Guess you missed me too much," he said.

"Yes, I miss you, and yes, I'm at the office, but that's not why I'm calling. Where are you right now?"

"What's wrong? Are you crying? I'm at the Versailles, having breakfast. In Little Havana, with my cousin. We'll be there in five minutes. What's going on?" he asked.

"Someone just threw a rock through my window. It just missed me."

"Maybe you better make a police report."

"I don't want to call. It's the Miami Police. They cover Coconut Grove. It might be the same guys who covered Lillian's case."

"So what? I'll be there with you by the time they arrive. They're not known for their swiftness. We're leaving now."

I had to stop calling Carlos every time something went wrong. This was out of character for me. I wasn't Snow White or Cinderella, and Carlos wasn't the Prince. I can handle anything, I thought, and then I began to cry again as I dialed 911.

Carlos was correct. He arrived before the police. A good-looking guy got out of the car with him. He was dressed in what looked like army fatigues and boots.

"This is Franco's brother, Marco," Carlos said, as I opened the locked back door for them. "I called the Glass Works. They'll be here in a few minutes to repair the window." He put his arm around me. "Let me see the damage."

We walked into my office. I saw the glass shards on my chair and desk, and I gasped when I realized the size of the rock. It looked more like a piece of a sidewalk, solid concrete with jagged edges. Marco started to pick it up.

"Leave it right there. The police are coming. They need to see where it landed and maybe they'll want to try to lift prints from it, although I doubt that's possible. The surface is too rough," I said.

"Marco does security work," Carlos said. "I'd like him to stay with you, until we find out if someone is trying to hurt you."

"What do you mean, stay with me? In my house or here? I appreciate it, but that's silly."

"I wouldn't be in your way," Marco said. "Just keep a watch outside your house and the office. The guys who work for me are trained to do surveillance."

Just then, the police car drove up. We saw one officer get out of the car and amble up to the front door. I opened the door and introduced myself. I saw from the nameplate that Jaime Frost was not an officer. He was a service aide. I guess a rock through a window doesn't qualify as a crime in this neighborhood.

I introduced Carlos and Marco, and pointed out the concrete "weapon" and the window.

"It's probably just kids," Jaime said as he examined the rock. "Is one of these guys your boyfriend? Had any arguments lately?"

Carlos's face turned red. I recognized that angry face. "Look, I'm Ms. Katz's boyfriend. Do you think I'd be standing around here if I was the rock thrower? Why isn't there an officer or a detective here?"

"Are you kidding? For a rock? There were two murders in the Grove last night. We're pretty busy. Was anybody injured here?"

"No, but I could have been. I had just been sitting at this desk. And a few days ago, someone slashed one of my tires in the parking lot here."

"Maybe one of your clients doesn't like you. You're a defense lawyer, aren't you?" Jaime smiled.

"No need to get sarcastic," Carlos spit out his words. "Are you going to write a report or not?"

"Sure, sure. I'll leave you a copy." Jaime returned to his car, and wrote for about twenty minutes. He left me a copy of the one-page report, and he left the rock without a backward glance.

CHAPTER TWENTY

Marco and his security guys were unobtrusive. I spotted their cars outside the office and the house over the next few days, but they faded into the background of the neighborhood. They stayed out of my way, and I did feel better having them around.

I glanced at my weekly calendar on Monday and realized that it was Jonathan's birthday on Thursday. That meant a full family dinner at my parents' house. The Magruder-Katz clan was big on celebrating birthdays, anniversaries, religious holidays for two religions, and other sundry occasions. I remembered promising my mother that I would bring Carlos to the next family dinner. This would be an endurance test for Carlos, meeting my parents, two brothers, their wives, and my four nephews in one noisy sitting.

"Thursday," Carlos said. "Thursday I'm supposed to have dinner with the guy who owns the Claremont Hotel. He's gonna hire me to convert the place to condos."

"Change the date. I went before the Marco Island

firing squad of Martins. Now it's your turn. I promised my mother. You don't want to start out with her hating you. Trust me. She holds a grudge for years."

Thursday afternoon Carlos picked me up at the office. We left before three o'clock to avoid the rush hour traffic, the after school traffic, and the usual over-turned semi on the turnpike. It's a ninety-minute drive to my parents' subdivision, which means it can take be-tween two hours and infinity. Jonathan, the birthday boy, and his family live on Miami Beach. His office is in a downtown Miami high-rise. William lives in Fort Lauderdale, close to his office. My retired parents live in Boynton Beach. However, in my family, the children are expected to spend all family occasions at the par-ents' home, not in restaurants near any of their work-ing children. They picture themselves somewhere between Ozzie and Harriet and the *Wonder Years*.

We were lucky to arrive by five-thirty. I had hoped to be there before the onslaught, but Jonathan's van and William's Lexus SUV were already in the driveway. The houses look like a village built out of children's blocks, each with its red-tile roof and tan stucco exterior, all facing the golf course or the man-made lagoons with spouting fountains.

I remembered the house I grew up in on Miami Beach. It was a rambling affair, with a screened porch across the back where my brothers and I sometimes slept in the summer. It was on a quiet tree-lined street when there were quiet streets on the beach, before the

South Beach glitz hit. Best of all, it was only a few blocks from my grandad's kosher market, where I could bring my friends after school for a cream soda. Now my nephews had to spend half a day in the car to visit their grandparents, and they probably couldn't pick out their house unless their car was outside.

Mother was waiting at the door for us. Her hair was pulled back in a French twist. She wore an apron over her pink and green pants outfit. If you looked in the dictionary under Wasp, beside the picture of the stinging bug would be a picture of my blue-eyed, blonde, Waspy mother.

She shook Carlos's hand and ushered us into the family room. My four nephews, two belonging to each brother, were engrossed in some electronic game. They ranged in age: thirteen, eleven, seven, and five. They yelled a collective "Hi, Aunt Mary" and went on with the game. Only Jake, the five year old, who really didn't get the game, came over and gave me a hug around my knees.

"Who's he?" he said pointing at Carlos.

"He's a guy who brings candy," Carlos said as he pulled a bag of gumdrops from his pocket.

Jake grinned and said, "I like him."

Carlos handed my mother a box of Perugia chocolates. She smiled too.

My dad and my brothers were on the patio looking at the pool. I introduced Carlos and there were handshakes all around.

"Do you play golf?" my dad asked.

"No, I really haven't had much time, but I do like baseball."

"No golf?" Dad looked at me accusingly. The conversation was at an end for him. Franklin was a golfer. Carlos had struck out.

My brothers were more cordial. They poured him a glass of champagne, our celebratory drink for all birthdays.

I went to the kitchen to look for my sisters-in-law. Randy, Jonathan's wife, was bending over the oven basting the brisket. She and Jonathan were very into Judaism. Their oldest was studying for his Bar Mitzvah. Joanie and William attended a Unitarian Church. I attended nothing. When people inquired, I told them I was a Druid and worshipped trees.

On the way to the kitchen, I passed through the dining room. The table was adorned with party hats and party poppers. Streamers hung from the light fixture. The decorations were the same as they were when we were grade schoolers. They never changed. Mother alibied that she did them for the grandkids, but I knew she wouldn't feel right without them.

Jonathan came into the kitchen, patted Randy on the tush, and came over to me. "I need to talk to you for a minute," he whispered and steered me out of the room.

We went into the bathroom. He shut the door.

"If it's about your birthday present, I actually have one for you. I was waiting til dinner." We sat down on the edge of the tub like we used to do when we were kids.

"Of course not. It's about the Yarmouth case."

"Oh, I guess I didn't thank you for sending Lillian to me. Sorry. It's a tough one, but I am grateful for the case. It'll keep the rent paid for quite a while."

"It's not about thank yous. It's something that's troubling me. I don't think this is going to violate attorney-client privilege, and I think you might need to know about this."

"Well, spill it. You look serious. Is it something bad about Lillian? Anyway, I'm not going to be reporting you to the bar. Whatever, it's just between us."

"You know I told you that I was Gary's estate-planning attorney. He revised his will last December. It wasn't a big deal, just to balance some tax concerns. He set up some additional trusts for his kids, and he put his house and condo in Lillian's name alone, took his name off of all his real estate."

"Why did he do that?" I asked.

"For tax purposes. It has to do with inheritance taxes, so when he died there wouldn't be any, and when Lillian died, the kids still wouldn't have big taxes facing them. It divides the estate so both husband and wife have equal parts of it."

"So, what's the point? What does this have to do

with Lillian's case? She wasn't going to get any greater benefit if Gary died, was she?"

"No, that's not it. Don't interrupt. You never have learned to listen," Jonathan said.

"I am listening. What?"

"After Gary's death, I got a call from a woman who wanted to know when Gary's will would be published. I asked her who she was. She said she was one of the beneficiaries, Maddie Rodriguez. I said I had no knowledge of her being a beneficiary. She became upset. She asked, 'aren't you the lawyer who revised Yarmouth's will recently.' I told her that I couldn't discuss my client with her, that if she had some proof that she was a beneficiary she should present it in person, and that if she intended to contest the will, she ought to obtain an attorney."

"Had you ever heard of her from Gary?"

"No, but something Gary said came back to me. He repeatedly told me he wanted to be sure that Lillian and the kids were protected. I told him he was doing the right things in his estate planning. I guess I just thought that he meant protected from Uncle Sam. You know, the tax ramifications."

"Did you ever hear more from this Maddie person?"

"Oh, yes. Two days after the phone call she appeared in my office demanding to see me. My secretary called me out of a meeting with clients. This woman was making such a fuss that my office crew was almost ready to call the police."

"Did you meet with her? What was she like?"

"I came out to the reception desk. She was screaming at Louise. You know what a good secretary Louise is, but she was having no luck shutting this banshee up. She was screaming at Louise, 'I don't give a fuck how busy this asshole is. He better get out here.'"

"What did she look like?"

"She was attractive in a cheap sort of way, long hair, tight pants, huge boobs. I led her into the back conference room and shut the door. I warned her that if she didn't quiet down, we would call the police.

"She said that she was sure that Gary had a provision in his will to take care of her. I asked her if she had any documents to back up her assumption. I told her that the will would become public in a few weeks and she would see for herself that she was not named in it. She called me a liar and said she'd make sure that I would be sorry for 'fucking with her.' She absolutely lost it. I thought she might be psychotic. I told her to get out of the office. She walked out of the conference room, and I called security. They escorted her out of the building. The whole thing was bizarre."

"Her name has surfaced more than once in this case. Please, this is confidential. Gary had a thing with her, and, when he was through playing, she wasn't. He couldn't get rid of her."

"Do you think Lillian knew and that's why she killed Gary?"

"I do not think Lillian killed Gary. I need to find Maddie Rodriguez."

Someone pounded on the bathroom door, and William yelled at us. "Jonathan, are you in there with Mary? How come I still get left out of the secret stuff?"

"Middle children always suffer," I reminded him.

The evening went pretty well. No one argued with anyone except about politics. Carlos and my nephews watched a soccer match on TV, and Carlos taught the older ones some Spanish soccer terms. This caused Mother to comment that Carlos liked children.

"Who doesn't?" he said.

Mother looked at me and said, "Some people don't seem to."

Jonathan opened his presents: a hideous tie from his kids, a new briefcase from Randy, a gift certificate to a South Beach restaurant from William and his family, two tickets to a Heat basketball game from Carlos and me (Courtesy of Carlos. I was too busy to shop), and a weekend stay at the Breakers Hotel in Palm Beach from my parents (their way of getting the grandkids for a weekend.)

Everyone headed for the door as soon as dinner ended. It was a school night. I went to the kitchen with Mother and Dad to help with the cleanup. Carlos was outside on his cell phone, which he had refrained from using during dinner.

"Carlos is a nice boy and good looking, too, and he's great with children," Mother beamed.

"But he doesn't play golf and he's probably Catholic," Dad said.

"Good night," I said and laid the dishtowel over Dad's arm.

CHAPTER TWENTY-ONE

The date for the preliminary hearing was closing in on me. I had to locate Maddie Rodriguez. I wasn't sure what I'd do when I found her. At the least, I'd interview her informally. If I could eyeball her, I'd be able to tell whether she was capable of being Gary's killer. I'm not the flashiest attorney around, but I am a good judge of character. When you make big mistakes about people, you learn. Look at the five years I wasted on Frank Fieldstone.

The day after Jonathan's birthday bash, I arrived at the office early. I had a new client to interview at the Federal Detention Center, but I wanted to get Catherine started on the hunt for Maddie.

"I want you to call each of the Omni Hotels in Miami and ask for Maddie Rodriguez. She was an event planner in one of them, and see if there's a corporate office in the area. Check there for her too."

"What should I say if I find her?"

"Nothing. Just hang up and I'll deal with her when I get back from the jail."

"What if someone asks why I want to talk to her?"

"They won't. Just say you're planning a wedding and she came highly recommended. I'm afraid she may be long gone, if she's the one who did Gary in."

I had time to berate myself as I fought the traffic on the way to the federal lockup. I put my name on the wheel in the federal court saying I would take court-appointed cases. These are cases of indigent defendants who cannot be represented by federal public defenders due to conflicts or because they are overloaded with work. When I opened my new office, I was afraid I wouldn't have enough work to pay the bills. Now I was on overload, but I couldn't say no. I might need the hourly stipend the feds paid at some later date, so here I was getting involved in more work.

I knew little about the case, just the name Fred Winslow, and the charge, trafficking in prescription drugs. A black man of indeterminable age was led into the attorney-visitor area. His hair was mostly grey and curled into a short afro. He walked slowly as if each step was painful. He smiled when I stood up and told him I was his new attorney.

"You know I can't afford to pay you nothing," he said as he settled into the chair across from me.

"That's not a problem. I'm paid by the federal court to represent you, Mr. Winslow."

"You can call me Freddy. You mean the government pays you? That don't sound like you're really my lawyer."

Well, Freddy, you'll have to trust me. Everyone is entitled to a lawyer in this country and if you can't afford one, the government pays for one. Remember, the cops probably told you that when they arrested you. Have you ever been arrested before? Whatever you tell me is strictly between you and me. That's called attorney-client privilege. I can never share it with anyone, unless you tell me I can."

"I was only ever arrested one other time, but that was twenty years ago, for driving with a broken headlight. Wasn't even my truck. It belonged to the cement yard where I was working at the time. But the cop pulled me in anyway. I got out the next morning. The judge threw out the ticket too. I guess the only thing I was guilty of was driving while black, as some of the young folks say."

"Okay, Freddy, tell me everything about this case. The charge says drug trafficking. At the time of your arrest, were you working?"

"No, I'm retired. I worked for Jack Reilly Construction for the last eighteen years. When I hit sixty-five, I got my Social Security and my Medicare. I was just tired of hauling and ladders and plaster and the whole bit. Millie, my wife, she retired a couple of years before me. She worked at Liberty School cafeteria for a long time."

"Okay, now tell me how you ended up here," I said as I doodled on my yellow pad.

"Well, Millie got sick two years ago. We thought it

was nothing, but she got worse and worse. The doctor told us it was colon cancer and that they'd do an operation. Then there was chemo, but nothing helped. I took care of her. The only thing left they could do was give her a lot of pain pills, oxycontin and morphine.

"Meanwhile, the bills started pouring in for the surgery and the chemo. I didn't understand. I spent hours on the phone trying to talk to Medicare. Finally, I went down to the Medicare office, and the lady explained that they only paid for part of it. She asked didn't I have some coverage from my job or Millie's job for the rest. Well, we never had no coverage. Millie was considered a part-timer even though she worked at the school forever, and Reilly never would pay for no health insurance, so there we were."

Freddie stopped and blew his nose. I could see the tears welling up.

"Did you talk to the hospital, Freddie? Did you try to work out something with them?"

"They was sending us letters that they were going to sue us if I didn't come up with some payment. I didn't want Millie to hear this. She was in so much pain. She died in August. I took out a mortgage on our house to pay for the funeral. It was all we had and we worked real hard to pay it off. I hated to start again, but I had to give her a good funeral. The church helped a little with it."

"I know this is hard for you, but can you get to how you got arrested?" I asked. I hadn't heard anything yet about a crime, except for the one the hospital committed dunning this poor guy.

"I thought the bills would stop when I told the hospital and the doctor that Millie was gone, but they said I still owed them for all of it. One day, I told my nephew that I thought I'd have to sell the house to pay the bills. He said maybe he knew someone who could help me get some money. He asked if I still had all those pills Millie had been taking. The next day this guy called me and said he was a friend of Tavaro's. That's my nephew. We never had no kids of our own. The guy told me to meet him at Myrtle's Bar, that's a little place in our neighborhood. He said bring him some of the pills Tavaro mentioned.

"I met him. I brought one bottle with me. He gave me five hundred dollars right there. He asked me how much more I had, and could I get more? Well, I remembered that I had a bunch of prescriptions and that some of the bottles said three refills on them. So over the next few weeks, we went around to different drugstores and got bunches of pills. I told him I didn't want no trouble. He said I wasn't the one selling them around and that I'd be okay. I got nine thousand dollars, and I made payments on the hospital bills, and then the DEA guys came to my house. They was a mean bunch, grabbed me when I opened the door. Told me I was under arrest and took me away. They questioned me for hours, but I told them I didn't know nothing, even when they said I'd get twenty-five years with no parole for drug trafficking."

"I understand everything now. It's true that these charges carry a twenty-five-year sentence, if you're convicted. If you're willing to cooperate by giving them the name of the guy who you sold to, I will work out a good deal for you. Possibly even probation since you have no prior record. Are you willing to give them information?"

"I don't know. That's being a snitch. He seemed like a nice kid."

"How nice is he, to let you take the fall for his drug business? And how do you know that he wasn't selling those pills to young kids who have become addicts?"

"I guess I didn't look at the whole picture. Give me a little time to think about it. Maybe you're right."

"You can call me collect and let me know if I can start some conversations with the drug agents or the prosecutor. Here's my card. And by the way, I want to see the hospital bills. We may have a civil case against them for charging you a lot more than they are allowed to. Medicare sets standard rates. You may end up being a rich man."

Freddy laughed. "That'll be the day."

CHAPTER TWENTY-TWO

I stopped at the deli and brought sandwiches for Catherine and me. Catherine had called the three Omni Hotels. The downtown hotel told her Maddie had worked there but had been transferred. They said they couldn't give her information about where she was working now.

"So I told them I was planning a wedding for five hundred people, and I would only deal with Maddie Rodriguez. They told me she was in their Palm Beach hotel, and even gave me her phone number."

"Good job, Catherine. How'd you like to take a field trip? Let's see if we can get her on the phone."

"I dialed the number and the extension. "Maddie Rodriguez. Can I help you?" the voice said.

"Yes, Ms. Rodriguez. My name is Catherine Aynsworth. You were highly recommended to me. I need help planning a wedding. My sister and I would like to come to see you as soon as possible. Today, if you can see us."

"Well, I'm pretty busy today. How about next week?"

"This is going to be a huge affair, over five hundred people, cocktails, dinner, an orchestra. We want to spare no expense, and guests will be coming from Europe and will stay at the hotel."

"Well, I could make time around four this afternoon."

"Great, we'll be there," I said.

"You're good at this," Catherine said as she applauded my performance.

"Sometimes good lawyering involves good lying," I said.

"Are we really going to pretend to be planning a wedding? Catherine asked as we drove up the interstate.

"No, that was just a ploy to get us in the door. I need to have two people there since I said you were bringing your sister. I don't want her to get suspicious and turn us away. If she's the killer, she'll be nervous about anyone she doesn't know. The fact that she quickly transferred to Palm Beach just adds to my suspicion."

"I thought Jack Brandeis looked suspicious when I was typing up your notes."

"I thought so too, but when I read the police report, there was a statement from a neighbor. The neighbor said a woman was seen running down the street in the vicinity of the Yarmouth house around the same time Lillian found Gary. The description said she had either blonde or red hair. Once we see Maddie, I'll go talk to the neighbor. No witness list has come from the state attorney yet, so I can still talk to the neighbor informally without deposing her.

"Once we get in the door, I have a plan. Just don't act surprised about anything I say. Take my cell phone out of my purse and keep it with you. It's a camera phone. I want you to snap some pictures of Maddie. Do you know how to use the camera?"

"They're all pretty much alike. I'll look it over. Won't she be suspicious if I'm snapping shots of her?"

"I'll keep her focused on me. Your job is to take a picture without seeming to take a picture. Got it?"

"This job is complicated, but it sure isn't boring," Catherine said, as she snapped my picture.

The hotel in Palm Beach was understated elegance. A uniformed valet took the car. He glanced disapprovingly at my old SUV, and brushed the dog hair from the seat before getting in.

"Any luggage?" he asked as he looked down his nose at us.

"No, we're here for a meeting, so we won't be long. Maybe you can leave the car in front. We may be in a hurry when we leave."

"I don't think my boss would like me leaving this car in front of the hotel," he said.

"I'm sure he wouldn't mind" I answered, and placed a couple of bills in his hand.

We saw him lock the car and place the key in his pocket.

The lobby was full of French Canadians gathered around the lobby bar. At the other end a large group sported name tags that said Brazilia '05. The din of French and Portuguese made it sound like we were in an airport in Europe. This was high season in South Florida.

We stopped at the concierge desk and asked for the catering department and were directed to the second floor

"Are you ready?" I asked as we approached the receptionist.

"It's your show," Catherine said. "I'm just the extra."

"Maddie Rodriguez, please. She's expecting us. Catherine Aynsworth."

We were directed to a waiting area. I busied myself looking through a copy of *Brides* magazine. After a few pages, I vowed that the only way I would get married was if I could elope.

"Ms. Aynsworth?"

I looked up and saw a young woman who personified the expression "A babe." She exuded sexiness from her low-cut blouse showing deep cleavage to her pencil-thin skirt slit to show long legs. What drew my attention the most was her mane of hair, which was strawberry blonde. It wasn't exactly blonde, and it wasn't exactly red. The color reminded me of the coat of a golden retriever.

"Is one of you Ms. Aynsworth?" Maddie asked again. We both answered.

"Please, come in," Maddie said. She led us down a hallway filled with tiny offices. She motioned us into one of them. I hung back and shut the door.

Catherine and I settled in two chairs so close that we bumped elbows. Maddie sat at the tiny writing table across from us. She pulled out what looked like an order pad.

"So, which of you is the bride?" she asked.

"Okay, Ms. Rodriguez. The truth is we're not here about a wedding. My name is Mary Magruder Katz. I'm an attorney and this is my assistant, Catherine Aynsworth."

I laid my card in front of her.

"What do you want? What's with the fake wedding business?"

"I was afraid that you wouldn't want to see an attorney, particularly one named Katz."

"Katz? Are you part of Jonathan Katz's law office?" Maddie stood up and leaned toward me. Her eyes looked furious. If stares could hurt you, I'd be lying on the floor bleeding.

"Jonathan is my brother, but we do not practice together or do anything else together either. I know you went to see him and that he told you that you weren't left anything by Gary Yarmouth. Gary didn't want anyone to know about you, so he didn't let Jonathan add you to his will, but that doesn't mean there isn't another will."

"I knew it," Maddie said as she sat down again. "No one dumps Maddie Rodriguez like yesterday's newspaper. Hey, wait, how do you know about this?"

"Remember, I'm a lawyer too. We have our networks. Let's just say, I know who else was involved in that will, but I can't reveal this yet. I have a conflict. I represent Lillian. Has the state contacted you to be a witness in her case?"

"They've subpoenaed me to testify at some hearing, but I haven't spoken to anybody about it yet."

"Excuse me, Maddie. Catherine, would you mind checking our phone messages at the office? Do you have your cell phone with you?"

Catherine had been sitting transfixed as if she were watching a TV soap. She had totally forgotten about the camera phone.

"Oh, yes, I'll do that right away," Catherine said and started rummaging through her huge backpack.

"Well, once Lillian's case is over, I can help you about the will. But if I do that now, it'll look like I'm trying to bribe a witness. Now let me ask you a couple of questions. When did Gary buy you that little red BMW, before or after you went to New York?"

"You know a lot. Gary must have talked to you. I get it. Okay, I can wait for you to show me the other will. He bought the car after New York. I'd been asking him for it for a while. I think that bitch, Lillian, must have found out about me and told him to get rid of me. And those brats of his; they had him wound around their fingers. But no one fucks with me like that. He was gonna buy me a little condo I had picked out, but—"Maddie didn't finish the thought. She looked angry again and punched her fist into her order pad.

"How's the new job going?" I asked. "You're not going to transfer again, are you?"

"Not for a while. I've put in for a European post, but they're hard to come by, and unfortunately, I don't have the ability to just quit. But maybe, with this other will—"

I interrupted her. "That's why you need to get in touch with me, if you decide to leave the area."

"You got that straight," she said.

"We've taken up enough of your time. Catherine and I need to get back to the office."

"Thanks for coming. I'll stay in touch," Maddie said.

We marched out of her office, took the stairs to the first floor, and beat it out of there.

Traffic was at its worst. It was Friday at five in the middle of high season. Drivers from a multitude of states and countries drove in a multitude of styles, some dodging in and out of lanes, others stopping cold to read the road signs.

"Let's get off of suicide alley and have dinner. Who's with your kids?"

"I'd love dinner. My neighbor agreed to meet them after school and they're actually going to sleep over with her kids," Catherine said.

We pulled off the interstate and into the parking lot at Pete's in Ft. Lauderdale. The happy hour bar and grill was just what we needed to relax.

"Did you get the pictures of Maddie?" I asked.

"Sure did." Catherine handed me the phone and I beamed up three excellent head shots.

"How did you know about the red BMW?" Catherine asked.

"I didn't for sure. The police report said a neighbor of the Yarmouth's spotted a young woman running down the street to a parked red BMW. The neighbor described the woman as having either long blonde or red hair."

"Wow, you hit pay dirt. This job is fun," Catherine said as she swigged down her second beer. It was two-for-one night.

CHAPTER TWENTY-THREE

It was after nine when I got home. I was pooped. Couldn't wait to take a shower and collapse in front of the TV. I hoped Sam hadn't punished me for being late with his dinner.

As I got out of the car, I heard Sam barking in the back yard. I had left him in the house. How did he get out? He is a wonder dog, but I doubted his ability to unlock doors. I went around to the yard. Sam was jumping on the back door and barking. He was panting heavily. He must have been out there for a while. We entered through the kitchen. I flicked on the light. No notes were near the phone. My parents and my neighbor had keys to the house. They would have left a note if they'd been there. I called out, "anyone here?" Sam ran to the living room, sniffing as he went.

I moved slowly into the dark room heading for the lamp by the sofa. The next thing I knew, I was on the floor. I must have tripped over something, but what? I felt around me and felt broken pieces of something sharp. Carefully I retreated to the kitchen, grabbed the flashlight by the back door, and returned to the living room.

My heart sank as I saw what was left of my cozy hideaway. There were only two possessions that I cared about in that room. I had inherited the rocker and the hooked rug from my parents' house. The rocker was the one each of us cuddled in with Mother when one of us was sick or scared. The rug was made by my grandmother. She brought it with her from North Carolina when my grandparents came to Florida. Everything else came from either the Goodwill store or yard sales.

The room was a jumble of broken items. I had fallen over the pieces of the lamp. The rocker was in pieces on the rug in front of the fireplace. I found the switch for the ceiling light. The light illuminated an ugly red stain covering the rug. The drawers of my desk were on the floor, their contents strewn over the broken pieces. I realized a burglary had taken place. But how had a strange burglar lured Sam into the backyard?

I hurried into the bedroom. I owned almost no jewelry except for the gold hoop earrings I was wearing. I didn't have the two-karat engagement ring anymore. The only other valuables were my Grandmother Katz's gold ring and a gold pennant my dad gave me for my sixteenth birthday. I opened the cubbyhole in my dresser. Both pieces were still there. Everything in the bedroom was intact, but there was another red stain on my flowered quilt. This was a bizarre burglary.

I sat down in the kitchen and caught my breath. Then I dialed the Coral Gables Police. I was not going to call Carlos, again. I didn't want him to think I was a helpless female; no, *I* didn't want to think I was a help-less female. If I kept having one trouble after another, I might scare Carlos away. That thought scared me more than the burglary.

While I waited for the police, I found Marco's card and called his after-hours number.

Marco answered after two rings. "Pit Bull Security, this is Marco."

"Marco, it's Mary Katz. My house was burglarized some time today. I'm waiting for the police now. Were any of your guys watching the place today?"

"Oh, geez, Mary, I'm sorry. We were only watching out for you, so Flako went by your office. When he saw you were gone, he figured you were in court. We never went by the house at all today. But Flako was going to pass by a couple of times later tonight. I'll get him to come by now."

"Flako? Which one is he?"

"The hefty guy who always wears the baseball cap."

"But flako means chicken. I thought that's what skinny guys are called."

"It is, but it's our little joke. The skinny guy in the office we call Gordo, which means —"

"I know. The fat guy. I'm not that big a Gringo. The police are here now. It's not your fault about this." I hung up and answered the door before Sam crashed through it.

The officers checked every part of the house. I couldn't find anything missing, just vandalized.

"I sent Officer Lewis to talk to your neighbors. See if anyone else has had an intruder recently, or see if anyone saw someone around your house," Officer Viejo said.

"Other than your parents and your neighbor, does anyone else have a key?"

"Not that I can remember. But I've had some other problems lately. Someone slashed one of my tires in my office parking lot and then someone threw a rock into my office window right where I was sitting. Officer, is that blood on my rug?"

"No, go over there and sniff it," he said.

"Ketchup! Someone poured ketchup on my rug and on my bed." I sat down on the floor and began to laugh. It was more like hysterics.

"I'll get you a copy of our report in the morning. This looks like vandalism. Any kids that you've had a problem with?"

"No, there aren't too many kids here. It's either older couples or younger professionals. I still can't see how someone came in here and lured my dog into the yard."

"Well, it looks like you've got a cleanup on your

hands, but you're lucky. You've still got your computer and your TV. The ketchup may even clean up out of your rug. Call us if you find anything missing, but I doubt we'll ever find who did this."

The officers rushed away to another call. I fed Sam and began to pick up the mess. The rocker was in three pieces. Maybe Donnie Robbins, the furniture restorer, could work on it. He was an old client from the Fieldstone firm. Then it hit me. Frank still had a key to the house and Sam knew him well. Frank also knew that the rocker and the rug had a history in my family. He also knew my weakness for fries and ketchup.

I went to the kitchen and found the empty ketchup bottle in the sink. My first call in the morning was to the locksmith to change the locks on all the doors

CHAPTER TWENTY-FOUR

Monday morning I went to the office early. I had a restless weekend. Even after the locks were changed. I felt uneasy. I mulled over what action to take against Frank. If I called the police and they arrested Frank for burglary, his legal career could be over. I didn't want to take away his law license, in spite of everything he was putting me through. He must have cared about me more than I had imagined.

I could request a restraining order to keep him away from my house and office. That would lead to a stalking charge. The news media would pick that up. I came up with a third way to deal with him.

My first phone call of the morning was to Marco and his Pit Bulls. I left him a message to stop by the office at his earliest convenience. Just as I ended that call, my cell phone rang. I didn't recognize the number on the caller ID, but I answered anyway.

"Mary Katz."

"Mary, it's Karen Kaminsky. I'm calling to remind you that our hearing before the bar ethics board is this week. I need to sit down with you. We have a lot of work to do to be prepared. Mary, are you there?"

"Yes, Karen. I guess I forgot about the hearing. There's been a lot going on here. Of course, I'll be available whenever you need me."

I had put the ethics hearing out of my mind. I needed the time to be ready for Lillian's hearing. If I didn't give Karen the time to help me, I could be out of business.

Karen and I worked long hours preparing our strategy. If I were found in violation, it could affect my ability to make a living. Karen asked me a lot of personal questions about Carlos. When she realized that she knew the Martin family, she asked to meet privately with Carlos. I wasn't sure what she was plotting, and I was terrified.

The night before the hearing, Carlos insisted on taking me to dinner.

"You're not eating and you're not talking," he said. "Think positive. I've been in a lot of scrapes, but the world turns and a new day erases the old. I think that's an old Spanish saying, but it doesn't seem to translate very well."

"Sure it does. You're used to getting into trouble and bouncing back. I'm used to getting people out of trouble, but this time I can't see how to get myself out of this."

"It'll be okay. Trust me."

"Oh, Carlos, shut up, before I start blaming you again."

The hearing before the Florida Bar Ethics Commission was held in the bar's Miami office boardroom. If the panel of three members were to find a possible violation, then they would hold a full hearing and forward a recommendation to the Supreme Court for punishment. This could be as little as a reprimand, or as big as a suspension or disbarment. This could be the first step in months of litigation and buckets of tears.

When we arrived at the bar's offices, I was shocked to see Carlos in the waiting area.

"What are you doing here?"

"Karen thought it might be a good idea." He smiled that heart-melting smile.

"Come on," Karen said, as she pushed me ahead. "Let me do my thing."

We entered the boardroom. A male bar counsel and two older panel members, both male, were seated at the table. No feminist friends here, I thought.

"Ms. Katz, you are charged with violation of 6-208 (d) of the Code of Professional Responsibility. This is a serious matter and, might I say, a rather delicate matter, as it has to do with your having sexual relations with a client right in your law office."

I felt my cheeks burning.

Karen began to speak. "Gentlemen, first let me present this group of letters from a number of bar

members attesting to the flawless record of Ms. Katz.
Next, I wish to present her record of activities to assist
the bar in its various charitable outreach programs,
most notably representing poor children who lack family ties and assistance. She has also served as a tutor and
mentor for children with learning disabilities."

"All very nice, counsel, but I don't care if she's
Mother Teresa. The point is, did she or didn't she get
caught diddling a client?" one of the old guys said.

"I'm getting to that. I know that we are not allowed to know who files the bar complaint against a
lawyer. However, we have reason to believe that this
complaint came from Ms. Katz's ex-fiancé, and is made
for vengeful reasons. If the saying goes 'hell hath no
fury like a woman scorned,' doesn't the same go for
the disgruntled rejected male?

"Now we all know," Karen continued, "that this
ethics rule was enacted over the objections of many bar
members. Some of you in this room posed the arguments against its passage. You asked what happens if
the lawyer is representing his or her spouse. Can they
no longer have sexual relations? We all know why the
rule was passed. It was because of one criminal defense
attorney who was sleeping with his client's wife. She
paid his fees with the idea in mind that her husband
would get life in prison and she'd be rid of him. We
can all see that is a conflict of interest. The committee
that fashioned the rule stated that where there is no
conflict of interest possible, there is an exception to

this rule. It is the client who must raise the complaint, because counsel took advantage of him. With that in mind, I am going to call Ms. Katz's client as a witness. Please, ask Mr. Martin to come in."

I was flabbergasted. Carlos entered the room. He looked professional in a conservative navy suit and white shirt. He also looked gorgeous.

Carlos was sworn in, and Karen began.

"State your name, please."

"Carlos Martin."

"What do you do for a living, sir?"

"I'm the owner of Martin Development Company."

"Say, young man, is your grandfather Jose Villa-Malado, on the board of the university?" one of the panelists inquired.

"That is correct."

"Well, I remember you when you were about five years old. You always were building something in his office, with boxes and ashtrays. So you're a builder now?"

"May I continue, gentlemen?" Karen smiled at the panel.

"Do you know the attorney, Mary Magruder Katz?"

"Yes, of course. She's my girlfriend. I am in love with her. And she's my attorney. And the best attorney I've ever had. Well, I mean ever hired."

I heard a few snickers from the panel.

"Now, Mr. Martin, have you been completely satisfied with her work on your behalf? That is, has she ever given you questionable advice or taken advantage of you because of your relationship?"

"Absolutely not. In fact, she tells me when I am wrong and makes sure that all my transactions are beyond reproach. In fact, I have been so impressed with her devotion to her profession, that I have just made a large contribution to the bar's foundation to aid children."

"Thank you, Mr. Martin. Does anyone have any questions for this witness?"

"Yes," said one of the three. "The complainant alluded to some ethical violations related to the transactions Ms. Katz has concluded for you, but there were no specifics. Can you shed any light on this?"

"I'm afraid not. Everyone I deal with makes money. They would hardly be complaining."

Karen took over. "If there are other allegations, we are unaware of them, and feel these innuendos are prejudicial to Ms. Katz."

"Counsel, don't get excited. I think I can speak for the panel when I say that this so-called violation is just a waste of time. It's clear that a family member can represent another family member. If you ask me these two look like they're going to become a family. Carlos is a nice boy, and I'm satisfied that this complaint must be dismissed. By the way, how much was that bar donation?"

"One hundred thousand dollars," Karen answered.

Karen had to prod me out of my chair. I was stunned. We left the room and the building and it wasn't until we hit the sidewalk that we all high-fived each other.

The last of the Franklin Fieldstone trumped-up litigation was over. I still needed to deal with his stalking before it escalated. Utilizing the courts would look like I was trying to manipulate the system just as Frank did. I hoped my plan of attack would work better than a police action.

I returned to the office to find Marco in the waiting room chatting up Catherine, who looked extremely interested in his every word. Well, he was a macho-type guy and she was single.

"Come on in, Marco. I have a job for you."

I explained my theory about Frank and why I didn't want the police involved.

"I know that Frank is a total wimp. He's terrified of physical confrontation when he might be the one getting hurt. Suppose that you or a couple of your Pit Bulls hang around and catch him in stalking mode. Maybe a little roughness would go a long way."

"You mean beat him up?" Marco looked surprised. "And how do you know he'll strike again?"

"Oh, I know he will. As soon as he finds out that I beat the ethics charges that he filed against me. He lost that one and his lawsuit against me. He can't stand to be beaten in court. I don't mean really beat him up. Just scare him a little. Like bend his left arm so he can't hoist his golf club. Maybe give him a black eye so he looks bad at the office."

"Okay, Mary, we'll do it. I can't say we haven't done similar in some divorce cases. A little threat goes a long way toward settlement. It works better than mediation."

"And one other thing, Marco. Don't tell Carlos about any of this. His Latin temper might cause him to try to remedy the situation in an inappropriate fashion."

"Oh, yeah. Carlos knows how to be inappropriate." Marco chuckled. "Hey, does Catherine have a boyfriend?"

CHAPTER TWENTY-FIVE

Lillian's hearing was scheduled for the following Monday afternoon. I was far from ready. The next four days would be 24–7 devoted to Lillian. I called Carlos and thanked him for saving my skin at the ethics hearing. I explained I would be working all week and weekend. He wasn't pleased, but he said he'd use the time to catch up on his own work.

"When you get through with her hearing, let's have a weekend away at the beach," he said.

"That sounds so good. I wish it were tomorrow," I said. "Dammit, now I can't concentrate."

The first person I needed to interview was Cassie Kahn, Lillian's neighbor, who had been mentioned in the police report. I enlarged the photos on my computer that Catherine took of Maddie, and set out for Bayshore Drive. I wanted to catch Cassie off guard, so I determined I would watch her house if she wasn't home. It's always better to catch a witness before they have time to plan their testimony. Once she talked to me, she couldn't change her story without blowing her credibility.

I rang the bell and was greeted by a tiny Guatemalan maid in full uniform.

"The Mrs. is outside. She love the sun."

She motioned for me to follow her. The pool and patio were actually on the side of the house. I wondered how Cassie could have seen so much from her backyard. Now I saw her clear view of the Yarmouth house and of the street, broken only by a few well-trimmed ixora bushes.

"Mrs., a lady to see you," the maid said.

Cassie got up from her chaise. She was wearing a very brief bikini. She was older than she appeared from across the lawn. She had a sculpted body that can only come from personal workouts at the gym. She wrapped a terry cover-up over the bikini, and glared at the maid.

"If you're selling something, I'm not buying," she barked at me. I was reminded of Sam's snarl at strangers who entered our yard.

"No, I'm not a salesperson." I handed her my card. "I represent your neighbor, Lillian Yarmouth. May I take a few minutes of your time to ask you about what you saw the day Gary died?"

"Oh, okay, I guess. Come on, we'll go in the house." She led the way through a side door into a library. "My husband loves to read," she said waving her hand at the bookshelves.

I noticed several legal volumes. "Is your husband

Jay Kahn? He works in the same firm as my brother, William."

"Yes, of course. Well, it's a small world, I always say. What can I do for you?"

"Would you mind if I turn on my tape recorder? It's easier than taking notes."

"Well, okay. The police officer who talked to me the day of the murder said I might be a witness, but you're the first one I've heard from since then. Maybe it'll be good to go over everything."

"I may need to subpoena you for a hearing," I said. I pulled the photos from my briefcase, but I kept them turned over. Cassie looked curiously at the backs of the pictures.

"This is just like *Law and Order*. I mean it's kind of exciting, being a witness. Do you think my picture will be in the paper? What do you think I should wear?"

"It's possible that the papers will cover the hearing, but you should wear whatever you feel comfortable wearing," I said. Cassie was ready to collect her fifteen minutes of fame.

"Now, let's go back to the day Gary died. Tell me what you remember of that afternoon. Even if you remember a small detail, it might be important, so don't hesitate to tell me everything you can think of about that day."

"Well, I saw Lillian that morning. She was watering her garden. You know she has a real green thumb. I called over to her to tell her how pretty everything looked, and she said she was glad because her kids were coming home for the long weekend. I told her Jay and I were giving a cocktail party that Sunday night and I told her they should all drop by. You know we always entertain a couple of the artists from the Grove Art Show."

"Okay, did you see Lillian any more that day?"

"That afternoon, I was sitting by the pool, just like I was today when you got here. I saw Lillian's car drive into the garage. It looked great, like she just got it washed or polished or something. She waved, and I waved back."

"Did you see her get out of the car?"

"No, I can't really see all the way into their garage, and she put the door down."

"Do you know what time it was when she drove in?"

"I know exactly, because I was waiting for a call from the caterer, for the party, you know, and she was supposed to call me at two thirty. She hadn't called and I looked at my Rolex. It said three exactly. That was right after I saw Lillian drive in."

"What else did you see?"

"Well, right after I looked at my watch, I started to get up to go in the house, and I saw this woman running down the street."

"What did she look like?"

"I didn't get a good look at her, just the side of her face, but she had this amazing hair. It was sort of blondish red. But the real reason I noticed her was that she stopped right near my yard and took off her shoes. They were those platform straw sandals. I guess she couldn't move too fast in them, so she picked them up and raced down the street towards the Hernandez's house. They're my neighbors on the other side."

"Did you see her do anything else?"

"She ran to a red 380 BMW and got in and revved the motor. I saw that car over there earlier and I wondered about it because Marlena and her husband were away in the Bahamas on their boat. I thought maybe they had someone doing some work on their house, but, trust me, this girl was no carpenter or maid."

"Now did you see or hear anything else?"

"I thought I heard a scream coming from the Yarmouths, but I'm not sure if it was from there or if it was kids outside somewhere. So I went in the house and a while later, the maid told me there were a bunch of police cars and an ambulance at the Yarmouths. Then the police officer knocked on our door and asked us some questions. I guess that's how I got to be a witness. Jay told me that I might have to give a statement and go to court."

Cassie almost licked her lips when she mentioned being a witness in court. She's probably the same type who rushes to get her picture in the paper at the charity balls. Lucky for me, she was enjoying her role.

"Cassie, will you look at these photos and tell me if you recognize the woman in them."

I spread them out in front of her. Catherine did a

great job. For blowups from a camera phone, they showed Maddie's face and unmistakable hair in some detail. Cassie looked at them for a few seconds.

"I can't say one hundred percent, but that sure looks like the hair on that girl running down the street. I think it's her. I wonder how she gets that color. Maybe we can find out who does her hair."

"What about the car? Had you ever seen it before around here?"

"Hey, there are a bunch of those little red BMWs all over the Grove, so I don't know if I ever particularly saw that one."

I switched off the tape recorder. "Thanks, Cassie. If you think of anything else, just call the numbers on my card. I appreciate your talking with me."

"It's my pleasure," she said as she walked me to the door. I saw the maid in the dining room, giggling into a cell phone, which she shoved in her pocket as we passed by.

CHAPTER TWENTY-SIX

I zoomed back to the office, and dived at my computer. I fired off a letter to the state attorney rescinding my request for reciprocal discovery. I still had no witness list from the state. Without their discovery, I wouldn't have to reveal my witnesses either. I could call anyone and the State would have no way to prepare for this hearing.

Catherine was gone for the day to her son's soccer game, but she had left a message on my desk in large red letters.

> A woman named Beverly called you. I guess it was the secretary at Elite that I remembered from your notes. She said it was urgent that you call her back. She left her cell phone number.

I glanced at my watch. It was five thirty. Maybe she'd be out of the office by now so she could talk. Beverly answered on the first ring.

"Hello?"

"Beverly? It's Mary Katz, returning your call. Can you talk?"

"Mary, can I come right over to your office? I need to show you something. I think it's important."

"Sure, Beverly, but it's rush hour. It'll take you forever to get here from North Miami."

"I don't mind. I need to see you."

"Tell you what. I'll meet you halfway. The bar at the Hyatt downtown."

"No. This is really private. Just wait there for me. I have your address on your card."

"Okay, sure. I'll be right here."

I decided to spend the next hour shaping up the witnesses and testimony I needed for the hearing. I also decided that I was starved. A quick call to Romano's Pizza Parlor for delivery took care of that. I sure needed an hour in the gym as soon as this hearing was over or I'd never get into my bikini for my weekend with Carlos.

Beverly arrived less than an hour later.

"You must have broken every speed limit. Here, I saved you a slice of pizza," I said, motioning her to a seat on the sofa.

"No thanks. I'm really too upset to eat," Beverly said. She opened a knitting bag she had placed on her lap and began pulling out some papers. "I could get in big trouble for this, especially if Jack finds out."

"I'll help you, I promise. Just explain to me what you've got."

"Well, Jack told me to go through Gary's papers. He told me to sort out company papers from his private correspondence. Jack said we had to prepare everything for the estate attorney, and for the company attorney. He told me to be sure there weren't any unpaid bills sitting around. Gary's desk and safe were filled with papers. I knew that he paid a lot of personal bills at the office. I found several bills from Bob Rose Investigation Service."

"Did you hear of that service before? Some companies use services like that to see what clients their competitors have. Did Elite do that?"

"Not that I knew of. These bills were sent directly to Gary at the office address. They're not addressed to Elite." Beverly handed over a stack of papers.

I looked through them. They were dated in December, January, and February, all recent dates. They were not itemized. All they said was "for services rendered," showing only the number of hours spent each month.

"When I opened the safe, I found a number of things. There was the price sticker and bill for a BMW. No one in the family or at the office drives one. There were other charge bills from stores in New York and hotels. Then I found this." Beverly handed me a large manila envelope.

I opened the envelope and pulled out a multipage report from Rose Investigations.

The first page was a letter signed by Bob Rose .

Dear Mr. Yarmouth:

You requested the services of Rose Investigations regarding background and activity of Ms. Maddie Rodriguez. Enclosed you will find a full report covering December 27 through February 3, 2005.

We are pleased to furnish you with the enclosed report. Should you desire further information on this subject or any other investigative work, please contact me directly.

Again, let me assure you, as I did by telephone yesterday, that all of our clients' matters are considered confidential. The only other copy of this report will be sequestered in my own file.

If you have any questions after reviewing my report, do not hesitate to contact me. Thank you for your business.

I opened the folder to which the letter was attached and began to read.

Final Report to Gary Yarmouth, Re:
Maddie Rodriguez, Latin Female.

February 5, 2005

At your request, we furnish the following information.

Background

Maddie Rodriguez was born in Havana, Cuba in 1977. She emigrated to the United States at the age of twelve, with her single mother. Father is unknown. They settled in Miami, living with cousins for two years, and later settling in Hialeah where Maddie completed high school. She attended Florida International University (FIU) where she received a degree in Hotel Management. She was employed part time at several restaurants and a Holiday Inn while she finished school.

For the past five years, she has worked for the Omni Hotel chain as a sales representative and then manager of their catering and special event department. She earns $45,000, per year plus commissions.

She was married briefly to Joaquin Serrano, a fellow student at FIU. His whereabouts are unknown. Their divorce was final in 1997.

In 1999, she was living with Bertram Olensky, who was manager of the Omni Hotel in Ft. Lauderdale. Mr. Olensky was 60 years old at the time and had been divorced for a year. We were unable to find the current location of Mr. Olensky. He resigned from his position with no notice in 2001. His former wife says she has not heard from him since early 2001. She was reluctant to give us further information.

We learned of another male involved with Ms. Rodriguez. In 2003, she was seen in the company of Morris Meier, Vice President of Ross Food Distributors. This was reported by another employee at Omni. We were able to locate Mr. Meier who has moved to Stuart, Florida, and has retired. He told us in confidence that he had a brief sexual relationship with Ms. Rodriguez, but ended the relationship after a few months. He said his wife became aware of the affair. He believes that Ms. Rodriguez told his wife of the affair. The

Meiers agreed to move from the area and are still married. He further stated that his affair was a stupid mistake and that he found Maddie to be somewhat unstable.

Surveillance of Maddie Rodriguez

We began watching Maddie's apartment on Coral Way in Miami on December 27. Most of her trips during the first three days were to work at the hotel. She remained at the hotel late into those evenings managing several holiday events. She was observed on her cell phone frequently while on the floor of those events. Our investigators infiltrated the parties, but because of the noise level were unable to hear her conversations.

On December 30 and 31, we followed Maddie to the Yarmouth residence. She parked across the street on both of those evenings and remained in her car, red 380 BMW, Florida tag # H 38 DC. We observed her using binoculars to watch the residence, and using her cell phone. She remained for two hours on December 30, from 9 p.m. to 11 p.m. On

December 31, she arrived at 8:10 p.m. and left when the Yarmouth family exited the residence in a white Lexus SUV. Maddie followed the vehicle to the Coral Bay Yacht Club and tried to enter the parking lot there, but was turned away by security.

On several occasions in January, we observed a Latin male enter and leave the apartment building of Maddie Rodriguez. An investigator followed him into the building and saw him enter Maddie's apartment. A check of his auto license plate came back to Reynaldo Francisco. Further investigation revealed that he is a busboy at the hotel where Maddie is employed. On January 4 and 5, he stayed until 7 a.m.

On ten occasions in January and February, Maddie was observed in the vicinity of the Yarmouth residence in Coconut Grove. On one occasion, on January 30, she was observed placing a letter in the mailbox at the residence at 1:30 in the afternoon. She was also observed at a condominium building at 5801 Collins Avenue in Miami Beach where a condo is owned by the Yarmouths, deeded to Lillian Yarmouth. She en-

tered the building on February 2 at 11
a.m., went to the fifteenth floor, and left
at 12:45. Security stated that she was
checked off a list of visitors at the security desk where residents notify the
guards who may be admitted. The
guards did not know who gave the approval.

Surveillance concluded as of the
writing of this report, per your instructions.

I put the report down and looked at Beverly. "This
is very important information. You were right to bring
it to me. Bob Rose will be a valuable witness at Lillian's
hearing. Let's make copies of the invoices so you can
return the originals to the office tomorrow. But I think
it best if you leave the report here. I don't want this to
fall into anyone's hands before the hearing. My tough-
est job is still ahead of me. I have to tell Lillian about
Maddie before she hears all of it in court."

"Oh, no. She may not be able to take it. She was so
devoted to Gary. Just to see them together was to know
how much she loved him. What do you think of Lillian's chances to prove her innocence?" Beverly asked.

"I think we both know who the killer is, and it's
not Lillian."

CHAPTER TWENTY-SEVEN

I telephoned Bob Rose at eight the next morning. I told his answering service that it was crucial I speak to him at once. He returned my call within minutes. I explained that I represented Lillian, and I needed his testimony at her hearing.

"I wondered when I would hear from someone regarding Gary Yarmouth's death," he said.

"You could have come forward yourself," I said.

"How could I? I didn't know what Mrs. Yarmouth knew or didn't know. All of my work is done with complete confidentiality."

"Of course, you're right. Thank goodness your report fell into my hands last night. You've had a good look at Maddie Rodriguez over several weeks. Do you think she could have been the one who killed Gary?"

"I can tell you one thing. She's a real nutcase. It's clear she was stalking Gary. He was very worried that she would ruin his marriage. He told me that he was committed to remaining married and that Maddie had been an expensive mistake. He was trying to cut his losses."

"Did he tell you what he intended to do about her after reading your report?"

"I assumed he planned to confront her. Maybe pay her off, or something. He said he couldn't go to the police without causing a scandal."

"What about all those other guys in her life? She was a busy girl."

"I think it was strange that I couldn't find a couple of them at all. It was like they just vanished, and if I do say so myself, I'm as good as a bloodhound at finding missing guys and gals. Maybe if I'd had more time, but Gary wanted to end the investigation after he read my report. I guess he knew everything he needed to know about his redheaded mistake."

We agreed to meet at the courthouse an hour before the hearing to go over his testimony, but I felt comfortable that Mr. Rose could handle any cross-examination by the state. He was a pro at being a witness, and besides, prosecutors never know how to cross-examine. They're used to presenting their case and having the defense present no witnesses. In the Florida system, the defense is allotted the first closing argument and a rebuttal argument after the state's close if they call no witnesses except the defendant. This is an incentive to call no one. Many cases are won by sparkling summations by smart defense attorneys.

Lillian's case would be won by hard work and preparation.

Something in Bob Rose's report kept rumbling around in my head. That condo on Collins Avenue. I had passed through security there when I visited Lillian after the murder. Gary must have agreed to meet Maddie there. What was the purpose of that meeting? One last day of lust? During working hours? It didn't make sense, especially because anyone could find out that Maddie had been there. Her name was on the list.

CHAPTER TWENTY-EIGHT

I told Catharine about Bob Rose. "Get Lillian on the phone for me. I've got to get her into the office today. She needs to hear this messy Maddie stuff from me before she hears it in court. See how soon she can come over. Tell her this will be a long session to prepare her for the hearing."

"Oh, boy, Mary, shall I run out to the store for more boxes of Kleenex?"

"No, just keep the coffee pot going and don't put any phone calls through unless it's an emergency."

"Even your mother?" Catherine was giggling as she went back to her desk.

Lillian arrived an hour later. I saw her get out of Sherry's sports car. I felt a surge of panic. Was she bringing Sherry in with her? I was nervous enough about telling Lillian the truth about Gary. I didn't want to be the one to break Sherry's heart too.

Lillian closed the car door and waved to Sherry who drove off honking her horn and blowing a kiss to her mother. Thank God, I would only have to deal with one hysterical woman.

Lillian looked more put together than any time since her arrest. She was dressed in wool slacks and a cashmere shell and cardigan. She looked younger and prettier. I was surprised to see how much calmer she appeared.

She was carrying a shopping bag with the Neiman Marcus logo.

"Mary, I'm glad to see you. This is for you," Lillian said, and handed me the bag.

I peaked inside. A thousand terrible thoughts rushed through my head, like maybe this was some secret evidence that would blow this whole case.

"Go on, open it. It won't bite." Lillian smiled at me expectantly.

I pushed aside the tissue paper in the package and pulled out an outrageously gorgeous Coach handbag. It was just the kind of purse I had always dreamed of owning, but never could splurge on.

"Lillian, this is beautiful, but what's it for?"

"It's for you to replace that black number that looks like a Goodwill reject that you carry around." She looked like one of those TV game-show hosts when the contestant wins the whole jackpot.

"No, I know what it's for, but why are you giving me a present?"

"Because I appreciate how hard you're working for me."

"That's what you're paying me for. We don't know yet how this case will turn out. Maybe you should wait before you start handing out rewards."

"I have great faith in you. Please accept this gift and use it well. You deserve it."

"Thank you, Lillian." I suddenly had a sick feeling in my stomach. I always get that when I realize how much a client is depending on me.

"Let's get down to business," I said. "We have a lot to talk over." I poured two cups of coffee from the carafe that Catherine brought in. "First, we need to review everything you said to the homicide detectives at your house and after they arrested you. Also, anything you said to the emergency medics. And try to remember exactly what you said on the phone when you called nine-one-one."

I decided to start with some fact gathering before I told Lillian the story of "the other woman." I wanted to be sure she could remember everything clearly. After I hit her with the bombshell, she might not even remember her name.

"It's hard to recall everything exactly. I was hysterical."

"Start with the phone call."

"Okay. I felt for Gary's pulse. There was nothing. I grabbed the phone on the nightstand. My hands were covered in blood and blood was on the phone. I think I said, my husband is bleeding. He might be dead. Come quick."

"Do you remember what the nine-one-one operator said?"

"She said to try to remain calm. She asked my name and address. She asked if I was in the house. I said I was. She asked if anyone else was there. I just kept telling her to get help there in a hurry."

"Who got there first, the police or the ambulance?"

"The medics. I let them in the front door and we raced back up the stairs. There were two of them. One tried to hear a heartbeat. He worked on Gary for a few minutes. He turned him over and we both saw the letter opener. He asked me what happened. I told him I didn't know."

"That letter opener. Is it yours? Do you remember where you last saw it before that day?"

"It's sort of an antique. It was my grandmother's. I kept it on my writing table in the bedroom. I think I used it that morning to go through the mail."

"Sherry told me that she thought it was stored in a drawer with the other family silver. Are you sure it was out on the desk?" I looked into Lillian's eyes.

"Of course, I'm sure. I wish it hadn't been there. Then maybe Gary would be alive."

"It's okay, Lillian. Don't blame yourself. Go ahead. You were telling me about the paramedic."

"Okay, I asked him why they weren't helping Gary. He said, 'I'm sorry, this gentleman has expired.'" Lillian paused. She started to cry.

"I know this is very hard for you, but we have to go over all of it." I put my arm around her and handed her some Kleenex. She shivered, and drew her sweater around her. "Lillian, when did the police arrive?"

"I looked up and there were two officers in uniform standing behind me in the bedroom. I don't know when they got there. I guess they just walked in. The medics told them Gary was dead, and they better call for detectives."

"Did the uniformed guys ask you any questions?"

"Oh, yes. One did all the talking. He asked me who else was in the house. I said no one. He asked me how I had gotten so bloody. I looked at my slacks and saw that I was covered in Gary's blood."

"Did anyone read you your Miranda rights? Tell you that you didn't have to talk to them and that you could have a lawyer present?"

"Not until later when the detective handcuffed me."

"What else did the uniformed officers ask?"

"They asked me how I was related to 'the deceased.' That's what they called Gary, the deceased. I said he's my husband. I think they asked if I had been in the house all day. I told them I just came home and that's when I found him."

"How long was it before the detectives arrived?"

"I think it was a few minutes. The uniformed officers told me not to touch anything, and they walked me downstairs to the living room. The medics came down and told me that they had to move Gary to the medical examiner's building for an autopsy. I wasn't sure I should let them do that. I asked if I could call my brother before they took Gary away. The officer said I didn't have a choice, that the medical examiner had been called and ordered that they bring him there. The officer said no phone calls until later."

"What happened when the detectives arrived?"

"They talked to the officers for a few minutes. Then one of them introduced himself. He said he was Detective Fonseca. He asked if I was Gary's wife. He said to tell him what happened. I said I came home and found Gary in the bedroom bleeding. He sort of insinuated that he didn't believe I had just come home. I said, go look in the kitchen where I had dropped my grocery bags, and look in the car where I supposed the rest of the stuff I bought was still there."

"You were getting the idea that he didn't believe you," I said.

"Oh, yes. He said that they checked the house and there was no sign of a break-in. He said the front door was unlocked and the alarm was turned off. I told him that when Gary got home he must have opened the door, and, of course, he had to have turned off the alarm."

"Did he ask you who else had access to the house?"

"No, he never asked that."

"Who else does have a key or comes and goes from here?"

"Our cleaning lady, Mabel. She's here on Monday, Wednesday, and Friday, but she leaves between one and two o'clock. The kids, when they're home. My sister-in-law has a key in case of emergencies. Since our dog died, we use the alarm more, but never if one of us is in the house."

"And you don't remember them asking about any of this?"

"I don't think they did. Oh, they asked about the blood on my hands and clothes. I told them that I must have gotten it when I tried to find Gary's pulse, and tried to see what had happened to him."

"When did they arrest you?"

"There were a bunch of people walking all over the house. They told me to stay in the living room. I asked if I could call my brother, that my children were arriving on a plane any minute and someone had to get to the airport. They wouldn't let me call. They said they'd call him. I gave them the number. I don't know how much time went by, but then Detective Fonseca came back in the room, and told me to stand up and put my hands behind my back. I asked him why. He said, 'because you're under arrest for the murder of your husband.' He handcuffed me. I was crying. I know he started to read me my rights. I told him over and over that I loved Gary, that this was all wrong. Then things went black."

"Did you faint?"

"I'm not sure, but the next thing I remember was

that I was in the police car. We got to the jail. The woman there told me to get out of my clothes. She had to give them to the police. She gave me a smock to wear, and they took me upstairs to a room full of women. Then you came to the jail to see me."

"All right, Lillian. Would you like to take a little break, maybe go to the restroom?"

"Yes, thanks Mary. I'm sorry I'm having a hard time remembering clearly."

"You're doing fine. Catherine will show you to the ladies' room."

I was the one who really needed the break. I was trying to get up my nerve to break the news to Lillian about her sainted husband. I wanted to see Carlos, and have a normal evening for a change. Well, evenings were not exactly normal with Carlos. They were more like every girl's erotic dream.

I decided that I deserved a minute to myself, so I dialed one of Carlos's cell phones. A strange voice answered, "Martin Development. This is Danny."

"Danny, where is Carlos? This is his girlfriend, Mary."

"Hi, Mary. Carlos had a little mishap or I guess you'd say misstep."

"Where is he? Is he okay?"

"I'm sure he will be, but right now he's at the Broward Memorial emergency room, getting checked out."

"What the hell happened?"

"He took a fall. He was up on the scaffolding at the new building and stepping onto the floor boards when the boards gave way."

"How high up was he?"

"About the twelfth floor."

"Oh my God." My heart was pounding.

"But he didn't fall off the building. He caught himself, and the guys working up there grabbed him. We think it's just his arm."

"Danny, if he calls, tell him I'm on the way."

As I hung up, I saw Lillian was back in the office staring at me.

"Lillian, I have to get to the hospital right away. I'm so sorry. Someone close to me has been injured. I hate to stop in the middle like this. I hope you understand." I was out of my chair searching for my car keys.

"Sure, Mary. I hope everything is okay," she said.

"I'll come over to your condo tonight as soon as I leave the hospital."

"That'll be fine. I'll fix a little dinner for us. Call when you're on the way."

I ran out of the office, told Catherine where I was going, and sped out onto Dixie Highway.

CHAPTER TWENTY-NINE

I took every shortcut I knew. I couldn't believe I had left an important client in the middle of her trial prep. It was time to face how much I had learned to care for Carlos. I couldn't even imagine how much he meant in my life. I didn't know if it was just the terrific sex, but whatever it was, for right now he was more important than work.

I raced into the emergency room. "Where can I find Carlos Martin?" I asked the receptionist.

"Is he a patient?"

"He was brought in a while ago. There was an accident at a building he was working on."

"Are you a relative?"

"No, I'm a friend."

"Well, we can't give you any information. Only family."

"I don't want information. I want to see him," I shouted.

"If he's being treated, no one is allowed back there." The receptionist turned away and answered the phone. She was clearly on a personal call, giggling and whispering into the phone.

I thought of another approach. She was still talking into the phone, but I talked over her, thrusting my card in her face.

"Look, I'm Mr. Martin's personal attorney. He told me to get right over here. He may have a lawsuit. I need to speak with him immediately."

The receptionist said into the phone, "Gotta go. Later." She examined the card. "Why didn't you say you were his attorney. Hank, show this lady back to exam room three," she said to an orderly standing nearby.

Hank pulled back the curtain. There was Carlos lying on a cot looking pale and uncomfortable. His long legs hung over the edge and his right arm was enveloped in a sling.

"Carlos, I got here as quick as I could."

"Mary." He turned toward me. He looked like a little boy who had been lost and just found his mommy. "Who called you? I told everyone not to let anyone know, especially you. I know how overworked you are right now."

"Don't be silly Carlos. There's no more important place to be than right here. I just figured that out. What did the doctors say?"

"They think it's a broken arm. We're waiting for the orthopedist to look at the X-rays now."

I pulled up a chair, plunked down and kissed Carlos hard.

*   *   *

Three hours later I was back on the road. Carlos had his arm set and placed in a cast. Franco picked him up in a van to drive him to my house to spend the night. I called Lillian and said I'd be right over.

The condo smelled of delicious food smells. I hadn't realized how hungry I was.

"No more work until you eat something," Lillian said as she met me at the door.

The dining room table was set for two. "Where are the kids," I asked.

"Gone down to the university. U of M is playing North Carolina tonight in basketball. It's a big game. I'm trying to get them back into their lives. They've sat around here long enough."

I was relieved that they wouldn't be around while we talked. Lillian returned from the kitchen with a quiche, a salad, and some hot rolls.

"I'm supposed to be taking care of you, not the other way around," I said as I tore into the food.

"You've looked out for me very well. I needed a break this afternoon, and cooking for a change was good therapy," she said.

As soon as we cleared the dishes, I said, "Let's get back to work now. You need to sit down. I have a lot to tell you, and you need to hear it from me before you hear any of it in court."

We sat down on the sofa. I remembered the last time I had been here. Lillian had been lying in shock on the same sofa. Now I was looking at an attractive, attentive woman. She leaned toward me with a look of curiosity.

"Lillian, I know how much you loved Gary. There's no good way to tell you this. Gary had been seeing a woman he met through his work. He realized it was a mistake and was trying to rectify what had become a problem. This woman turned out to be unstable. Gary hired an investigator to watch her. Perhaps you should read the report. It shows that Gary was trying to get rid of her. I have reason to believe that she may have been the person who killed Gary. She was seen stalking him. The investigator spotted her in the vicinity of your house on more than one occasion."

I paused and looked at Lillian. She didn't budge. She wasn't crying. She looked completely unperturbed. She leaned over and patted my arm.

"I know all about it, my dear. Gary was a very poor liar. This woman wasn't the first. Gary was what we call a lady's man. I knew there was some new plaything when he went to New York and didn't invite me. That was always a sign. I took most trips with him."

I was stunned. "But everyone tried to keep this from you."

"Who is everyone?"

"Well, Marian and Jack, and Brett."

"I didn't know that Brett knew. Jack would never let me know he knew something that would hurt me. He never understood why I married Gary or stayed with him. He disliked Gary from the first minute I brought him home. I'm concerned about Brett. He adored his dad. I don't want the children to have their hero taken away from them."

"Brett will be okay, but someone will have to tell Sherry so she isn't shocked at your hearing. I'll be putting Bob Rose on as a witness. He's the P.I., and his report will be introduced. The state may call Maddie Rodriquez to testify. She's the woman Gary was seeing. Lillian, it's none of my business, but why did you stay with Gary, if he ran around on you?" I realized that I sounded like my mother, asking such a question.

"It's not complicated. I loved him. He was exciting and fun, always full of ideas. I liked my life. We played golf, went out on family outings on the boat, went to great parties. I liked being the attractive couple that others envied."

"Weren't you ever fearful that he would leave you during one of his extracurricular affairs?"

"No way would he do that. I own the controlling shares of Dad's company. Gary had the title, but I owned the stock. I could have fired him whenever I wanted and he'd be out of a job and out of the lifestyle he wanted. I knew he loved me. I also knew he loved the life I gave him. So I was never worried."

"Was Gary aware that you knew about Maddie?" I asked. I was still groping for some clue to this very different person that Lillian had become. It was like watching a butterfly emerge from the cocoon that once covered a caterpillar.

"Yes, he knew. You see, someone wrote me a letter telling me that Gary was having a thing with a young woman named Maddie Rodriguez. I showed him the letter. He was grief stricken. He told me that he had broken it off with her and that she wouldn't leave him alone. He begged me not to leave him, that he would make sure that none of this would hurt me. He said he couldn't believe how stupid he'd been to become involved with her."

"Do you still have the letter?"

"No. I threw it away. It was not the sort of thing one would want lying around the house."

"Do you know who wrote it?"

"I don't know, but I suspect it was the woman herself."

"That would fit with what I know about her. She's a sicko. She probably thought you'd leave him if you knew. There were a number of other men that she preyed upon. It's all in that report."

"Do you really believe that she killed Gary? You mean she was in my house?" For the first time that evening, Lillian looked angry. "How did she get in? Gary couldn't have brought her into our house."

"I know she was seen by a neighbor running away from your house right after you drove into the garage, so, yes, I guess she was in your house. Bob Rose's report said she was spotted spying on your house. She was definitely stalking Gary. Maybe she followed him home and he let her in, or, maybe she found the door unlocked and walked in. What I find most egregious is that the police didn't do anything to investigate."

"I always thought someone broke in. There have been so many burglaries in the Grove. I figured the police had let any clues go cold, but once you were representing me, I just had this feeling you would find out the truth. I was right."

Brett and Sherry came in just then, and after a few minutes of small talk, I left. The ride home went quickly. I was engrossed in replaying the whole conversation with Lillian. Behind her delicate façade was a dragon. The golden tea rose dropped her petals and was all thorns.

I tiptoed into the house. Carlos was sitting up in bed. His cast was propped up on some kind of gizmo that Franco must have fashioned.

"You are wide awake," I said. "I thought you'd be out on pain pills."

"I waited to take them until you got here."

"Can I get you anything?" I asked leaning over the bed.

Carlos pulled me into the bed with his one good arm. "Yes, you may remove your clothes," he said.

It's amazing what that guy can do with only one arm.

CHAPTER THIRTY

Sunday afternoon I moved Carlos back to his house. He was doing well enough to be on his own. His employees were lined up to drive him to his office on Monday, and he promised to stay off the construction sites for at least a week.

I had gotten some work done while Carlos vegged out on pain pills. The rest of Sunday was spent going over every part of the upcoming hearing. My push to have a preliminary hearing was to illustrate the fact that the State had no evidence against Lillian. The State always puts on its case first, because they have the burden of showing that a crime has been committed and the defendant is the person who committed the crime. In a trial, their burden is to prove their case beyond a reasonable doubt. At the hearing, their job is to show that there is enough evidence to support the charge they have filed against the defendant. Everyone knew a murder was committed. My job was to destroy the feeble case the State had against Lillian.

Our justice system is never supposed to place the

burden of proof on the accused, but in reality the defense is always on the spot to plant a doubt in the mind of the judge or the jury. In Lillian's case, the State was going to be able to prove nothing except that the police failed to investigate Gary's murder. I would be able to show the court who the real killer was. I was gambling that Lillian's case would be dropped at the end of the hearing.

I decided that I had done all I could do to be ready for the hearing on Monday. I packed my brief-case and boxes, and fell into bed before eleven.

I don't know how long I was asleep when I was awakened by the sound of voices shouting and the doorbell ringing. A doorbell is an unnecessary addi-tion when you have a large dog. Sam's baritone bark al-most drowned out the doorbell. I leapt out of bed and peered out the window. I saw car lights everywhere.

Sam and I approached the front door gingerly. "Who is it? What do you want?" I shouted.

"Mary, it's Marco. Open up."

I threw open the door. Marco and one of his Pit Bulls were holding a bloody Franklin Fieldstone. An-other of the beefy Pit Bulls was standing behind them.

"We caught him in the act, Mary. The dumb bas-tard was trying to fit a key into your front door. We had to rough him up a little. He resisted our assistance in removing him from your front step," Marco said wink-ing at me.

Frank was dressed in black slacks and a black tee

shirt. His nose was dropping bloody pools down the front of the shirt.

"Isn't the hour a bit late for paying me a visit?" I said. "So it has been you that turned into a stalker."

"You tell these bozos to get their hands off me or I'll call the police," Frank said.

"Oh, yeah, good idea. Then we can report Mary's slashed tire, broken window, and vandalized house. They'll enjoy charging a high-priced lawyer with burglary," Marco said.

"Frank, why are you doing this? You know I could report you to the police and see that you're charged with multiple felonies. Why would you risk your reputation?" I asked.

"Well, obviously, because I care about you," Frank said.

"Some way to show you care," Marco said as he gave Frank's arm a good twist.

"I think what you really care about isn't me. It's that you couldn't get your own way for once. A good lawyer left your firm and beat you in court and in the ethics proceeding. You just can't stand to lose at anything, and to be beaten by a mere woman was just too much. Maybe calling the police is a good idea," I said. "Marco, go ahead and call Coral Gables P.D."

"Now wait a minute," Frank said. For a minute, I thought he was going to cry.

"Look, buddy," Marco said, "if you will cut out this crap and leave Mary alone, we'll let these criminal acts slide for now. But if you so much as come near her again, Mary will file charges. My employees and I will be watching. Before you go to jail, you'll need a trip to the hospital. Got it?"

"I can't believe you'd hire a bunch of guys like this," Frank said.

"Well, I can't believe you'd turn into a common stalker," I said. "Are you going to agree to leave me alone?"

"If that's what you want, okay then," Frank said.

Marco escorted Frank to his car, which was parked across the street. Sam continued to growl until the car pulled away. Then I invited Marco and the Pit Bulls in for a celebratory beer.

CHAPTER THIRTY-ONE

Monday morning arrived with the clock radio announcing that it was six a.m., and that a heavy fog covered all of Miami-Dade County. My head was certainly in tune with the weather. Fog covered my eyes and brain. I took Sam for a run to the Miracle Mile, ordered the strongest cup of caffeine at Starbucks, and grabbed the morning *Herald*.

The headline shouted SUSPECTED SPOUSE KILLER AWAITS HEARING. A picture of Lillian and me leaving the courthouse after the last hearing exploded under the headline. I looked like a self-satisfied cat with a mouse in tow, and Lillian looked like the mouse. I had her by the arm as she cowered from the photographers. No one viewing that photo would believe she was a killer. I hoped Judge Arnold read the paper before court. Most judges do, to see if their name is there or if their colleagues are getting more publicity than they are. This is a product of judges being elected every six years.

The article reviewed the murder and the background of the players: prominent family, CEO of local company, well-known charitable givers. Nothing harmful to Lillian, and no mention of Maddie. The good part of practicing law in Miami is that there are so many murders and corruption trials that the paper doesn't have time to dig into each one.

I returned home to shower and do my hair. I decided on a white suit. White always denotes the good guys and it's also the color choice of the Santerias, the Cuban religious group based on voodoo and magic. Not that I'm superstitious, but it's best to cover all the bases.

Catherine had more coffee ready at the office. "Brett called early to see if you were picking them up again," she said. He sounded a little rattled. I didn't know if you'd have time to go all the way over there, so I called Marco's security office and asked them to provide a car and driver. The Yarmouths can certainly afford it. Lillian's been paying your fees the instant she gets the bills. Was it okay that I arranged the car?"

"That was good thinking. It gives me more time to go over everything in my trial boxes. Let's make sure that I have every folder for each witness. Do I have a time set to speak to each of them before the hearing?"

Catherine handed me the list. "I reserved the attorney interview room on the third floor like you asked, and all the witnesses know the room number."

"Good. We'll keep them away from the courtroom

until I call them to testify. You'll be in charge of moving them up to the sixth floor. This'll be a real help."

Catherine was excited about being on the scene. I noticed that she had tied her hair back and was wearing a pantsuit for the occasion instead of her usual jeans and sneakers outfit. But she still had the humongous backpack that went everywhere with her.

We loaded the boxes of notes and witness folders into the SUV along with the box of yellow pads, pens, paper clips, and an envelope with the photos of Maddie.

"What do you have in that backpack?" My curiosity took precedence over good manners.

"Oh, just a few things. Power bars, a water bottle, some pictures, cookies that I baked last night, some good-luck charms. Just the usual kind of stuff," she said.

I smiled at this wonder woman. There was nothing usual about Catherine.

We arrived at the courthouse two hours before the hearing, well ahead of the press. Catherine and I loaded our boxes onto a wheely cart and got them into the attorney interview room. Then we went back down to the front entrance to meet Lillian and her kids.

Marco's black SUV pulled up to the curb. I was surprised to see that Marco himself was the driver. He hopped out and helped the Yarmouths out. While I was shaking hands and kissing cheeks with Lillian and her kids, I realized that Marco was having a whispered chat with Catherine, who was blushing. Maybe the reason for Catherine's attractive outfit wasn't for her apearance in court, but for being courted by the head Pit Bull.

I led Lillian into the courthouse followed by Brett and Sherry. Catherine brought up the rear. We hurried them upstairs to a witness waiting room out of the reach of the press and public. It was almost time for the show to begin. I was running on nervous energy. I couldn't imagine how Lillian could look so cool. She seemed totally calm. It could be a show for her children, or maybe she was used to stifling her emotions. Her appearance was completely different than it had been in the weeks right after Gary's murder.

Promptly at one-thirty, Lillian and I took our seats at the defense table. All four prosecutors crowded around the State's table. They huddled together whispering. They were shocked when Catherine and I wheeled our boxes and files into the courtroom and began assembling the witness folders on the table behind us. The State appeared to have only one small box of papers. I had to choke back the urge to laugh or high-five Catherine. They hadn't done their homework.

Judge Arnold took his seat on the bench. "Good afternoon, State and Defense. Are all parties ready to proceed with the preliminary hearing?"

"Yes, Your Honor," I said. "I would like to introduce my paralegal, Catherine Aynsworth. May I have the court's permission for her to assist me this afternoon? She will be helping me with my files, and bringing my witnesses into the courtroom."

The judge nodded his assent.

"Witnesses, Your Honor?" Karl Morris was on his feet, his voice rising to a high squeak. "The State was never informed of any witnesses."

"Well, Your Honor, I revoked my demand for reciprocal discovery. The State dragged their feet so long in turning over any witnesses or documents that I decided to forego discovery, so I don't know who their witnesses are either," I paused to take a breath.

"Judge, we sent her the initial police report."

"I could have gotten that on my own, Judge. That brief report was all I ever got."

"Okay, Counsel, looks like we'll all see the witnesses together in a few minutes," Judge Arnold said. "State are you ready to proceed with your first witness?"

"No, Your Honor. Ms. McIver, who is the case-law expert on our team, wishes to argue a motion, objecting to having a preliminary hearing in this case." Lois McIver got to her feet and headed toward the lectern. She was carrying a stack of cases.

I was on my feet before she made it to the lectern. "Judge, this motion is too late. Today is the day of the hearing. The State has had over three weeks to file and argue such a motion. Additionally, I have several cases to pass up to the court showing that Mrs. Yarmouth has every right to this hearing, especially in light of the fact that no discovery will be exchanged."

"Ms. McIver, have a seat. I have researched the law in this area myself. I am satisfied that I have made the right decision. You have had ample time to appeal my decision. You haven't done so, so let's get on with the hearing. How many witnesses will you be calling, Mr. Morris?"

"Probably two or three," Morris answered.

"And you, Ms. Katz?"

"About the same number, Judge."

"Then let's get going. I like to have dinner before breakfast. State, call your first witness."

"The State calls Detective Harry Fonseca."

The bailiff went through the double doors into the hallway and bellowed for the detective. He entered behind the bailiff, walking with a slight swagger. He was dressed in his best courtroom apparel, dark pin-striped suit, white shirt, red tie, all of which covered his tattoos.

While the clerk was swearing in the detective, a young woman entered and motioned for one of the prosecutors to approach. I recognized her as one of the secretaries in the state attorney's office. Charlene Montavo came to the bar that separates the public area from the well of the court. The secretary handed her a note. Charlene read it and dashed over to Karl, who was at the lectern ready to begin his questioning. Karl looked at the note, frowned, wrote something on it, and Charlene rushed back to the secretary who hurried out of the courtroom.

Catherine was seated beside me. "Go out and see if you can find out what's up with the State," I whispered. She moved out right behind the State's secretary.

Karl looked confused. He shuffled his notes and began questioning the detective.

"State your name and occupation, sir."

"Harry Fonseca, detective, Homicide Division, Miami Police Department."

"And how long have you been so employed?"

"I've been with the department eight years. I was a patrol officer for two years, a general detective for one year, then I was assigned to robbery for three years, and two years ago I moved to homicide."

"Have you received any special education for your position?"

"I graduated from the police academy eight years ago, and I took a fingerprint course three years ago."

"Were you assigned to investigate the murder of Gary Yarmouth on February 8th?"

"Yes, I was assigned as the lead investigator."

"And what duties does the lead investigator have?"

Judge Arnold interrupted. "There's no jury here, Mr. Morris. I don't need to hear an explanation of what work the police do or don't do. Just get to the meat of this thing."

"Yes, Your Honor. Detective, when did you arrive

at the Yarmouth residence and what did you observe when you arrived?"

I got there around four fifteen or so. I talked briefly to the first officers on the scene. They had placed Mrs. Yarmouth, the defendant, in the living room. She was seated on a sofa, crying. Her clothes were bloody. There were no signs of a break-in. The front and back doors were unlocked and the alarm system was disengaged. I went upstairs and saw the deceased lying across a bed. One of the officers handed me an evidence bag containing a silver letter opener with a six-inch sharp blade."

Karl picked up a plastic bag and brought it to our table.

"Any objection to the introduction of this letter opener?" Karl asked.

"It's fine. No objection," I said, standing up, hoping to shield Lillian's eyes from the weapon.

"Okay, Counsel. It's entered," said Judge Arnold.

"State's exhibit one in evidence," the clerk said as she stamped the evidence bag.

"Was anyone else present in the house?" Karl continued his questioning.

"Just the officers. The emergency medical personnel had already left. The people from the medical examiner's office arrived shortly after I did. They made some notes and removed the body."

"Did you talk to the defendant?"

"Of course. I asked her if she had been home all

day. She said she had been out shopping. I asked her if she and her husband had been arguing. There was a chair overturned in the bedroom. She kept saying that she loved him. I asked her who owned the letter opener. She said it was hers, that it had been her grandmother's. I asked her where she kept it. She said on her writing table in the bedroom."

"Were you able to find any other witnesses to talk to?"

"One of the officers spoke to a neighbor, I believe. May I look at my report? I can't remember who that was, but I do remember that it didn't lead us anywhere."

"You may refresh your recollection from the report."

Detective Fonseca glanced through some papers. "Oh, yes, the next door neighbor claimed that she saw Mrs. Yarmouth drive into her garage that afternoon. She also saw a woman walking down the street, but she got in a car parked two doors away."

"What else did you do that afternoon?"

"I arrested Lillian Yarmouth and charged her with the murder. It was a clear open-and-shut case. She was taken to the women's detention center."

"Now did you do any further investigation in the case?"

"Yes. I talked to people at the deceased's place of business and I examined some credit card bills and phone records belonging to the deceased. There were hotel bills in New York and locally. There was also a telephone number called numerous times on his cell phone. We retrieved the name of the person whose number was called. It belonged to a woman named Maddie Rodriguez. We located her and my partner and I interviewed her. She admitted that—"

"Objection, Your Honor. This is hearsay," I said.

"Well, it's part of his investigation," Karl replied.

"Judge, it doesn't matter what it's part of. It's still hearsay. It's what someone said outside of this court-room."

"It is hearsay, Mr. Morris. Does it fall under any exception to the hearsay rule?" Judge Arnold asked.

"May we come sidebar?" Karl asked. He looked agitated.

The judge nodded and gestured us forward. We gathered around the judge and the court reporter.

"I have a slight problem," Karl whispered. He gestured for the other prosecutors to join him.

"It must be more than a slight problem, if Mr. Morris needs to call out this army," I said.

The judge smiled. "What is the problem, sir?"

We were prepared to call Ms. Rodriguez as a witness today, but we have been unable to locate her. My co-counsel have been checking with our investigator to see if she has been located. That's why I called them up here."

Charlene Montavo stepped into our huddle. "Your Honor, we have been on the phone with the investigator. He has checked her work and her home and no one has seen her since yesterday. We are searching for her car and any other clues to her whereabouts, but at this time it seems she is unavailable, or has made herself unavailable."

"So, Judge, her statements would fall under the exception of unavailability, and I could then inquire as to what she told the detective," Karl said.

"I have no objection to this as long as I am afforded the same leeway in questioning my witnesses and cross-examining their witnesses," I said.

"Okay, done," said the judge. "Proceed, Counsel."

"Detective Fonseca, what did you learn when you interviewed Maddie Rodriguez?"

"She admitted to having an affair with Gary Yarmouth over the preceding months. She further stated that she was sure that Lillian Yarmouth knew about the affair, and had been trying to get Gary to break it off, but Gary was committed to continuing the romance and divorcing his wife."

"Did you do any other work in this case?"

"Other than writing some reports, no. We were sure that we correctly closed this case."

"Thank you, Detective." Karl took his seat.

I moved to the lectern, ready to cross-examine the detective, just as Catherine hurried back into the court room.

"May I have a moment with my paralegal, Judge?"

I moved back to the table where Catherine whispered to me, "Maddie Rodriguez has disappeared. The

State is going nuts trying to find her. I overheard the secretary on her cell phone with someone, it must have been one of their investigators. It sounded like he went to Palm Beach to pick her up for court and she was gone."

"I just found that out. She must have split before she got charged with the murder," I said. Catherine and I looked at each other and smiled.

"Detective Fonseca, did you ever follow up with the neighbor who saw a woman running away from the Yarmouth house?" I began my cross-examination.

"Well, no, I read the patrol officer's notes, and it didn't seem important."

"Did you find out what type of car the runaway woman drove off in?"

"I'll have to look at my report. Offhand, I don't remember. Yes, a small red car."

"Did you ever check to see what kind of car Maddie Rodriguez owned?"

"I don't believe I did. I might have."

"Well, did you or didn't you?"

"I have no recollection of checking the car."

"You stated that Mrs. Yarmouth told you she had been away shopping, came home, and found her husband bleeding in the bedroom. Did you check in any way to see if what she told you was true?"

"I saw some bags of groceries in the kitchen, and some packages were found in her car, but they could have been there for hours or even days."

"Well, was some of the food decomposing or was there melting ice cream?"

"Not that I recall."

"Did you ask for the names of stores Mrs. Yarmouth had visited? Did you check the receipts in the packages?"

"I don't believe I did. Maybe another officer did."

"Wouldn't finding out the times Mrs.Yarmouth visited the stores have either confirmed her statement or discounted it?"

"Possibly."

"By the way, did you read Mrs. Yarmouth her Miranda rights before questioning her?"

"Of course."

"May I see the waiver of rights form you had her sign?"

"I didn't give her a written form. I just read her the rights form."

"Did you note the time of the reading of the rights form?"

"I'll have to look at my report."

"Certainly, go ahead."

"I'm having a little problem finding the time."

"It's true, isn't it, Detective, that you didn't inform her of her right to remain silent and to have her attorney present until after you spoke to her and were in the process of arresting her?"

"I do see a notation that I Mirandized her at the time of her arrest."

"Did you ever ask Lillian who else had access to the house?"

"I didn't ask her. Maybe another officer did."

"What about fingerprints on the letter opener? Were prints recovered?"

"There were numerous smudged prints all over the handle. There were only partial prints, not enough points to make a match."

"What about the blood on Lillian's clothes? Was any of it her blood?"

"No, the blood was from the deceased."

"Were there any signs that Lillian had been involved in a struggle or a fight?"

"Not that I can recall."

"So based on the fact that Lillian Yarmouth was the only person in the house, you charged her with murder, with no fingerprints, no follow-up with her neighbor, no investigation of where she had been that afternoon, and no idea of who else had access to the Yarmouth residence? Is that correct?"

"Objection, Your Honor." Karl was on his feet. "That is a compound question and Ms. Katz is badgering the witness."

"I'll withdraw my question, Judge, and that concludes my cross-examination of this witness."

"I have just one redirect question, Judge," Karl said. "Detective Fonseca, did you have any doubts about whether Lillian Yarmouth was the murderer of her husband?"

"Certainly not. I have a good gut instinct regarding the perpetrators of crimes."

I was on my feet. I was furious with such a ridiculous answer. "Your Honor, I know I'm not entitled to a recross, but this answer triggers a new area. May I ask a couple of questions?"

The detective was about to leave the witness chair, but Judge Arnold motioned him to stay put. "Go ahead, Ms. Katz, and bailiff, cancel the other hearings for this afternoon. This one is going to take a while," the judge said.

"Detective, you've been working homicide cases for three years, correct?"

"Yes, three years."

"It's correct that you take great pride in your work?"

"Of course."

"That would include closing cases based on thorough investigations, right?"

"That's what I do."

"But in this case you failed to investigate several areas and, as you just told Mr. Morris, you relied on your gut instinct to arrest Lillian Yarmouth?"

"What I meant was I see a lot of people and I can judge when they're guilty."

"Well, if you can do the judging, there's no need for a court of law is there, sir?"

The detective's face turned a lovely shade of red, as I gathered my notes and sat down.

"You're excused, Detective Fonseca," Judge Arnold said. "Let's take a five minute break."

Judge Arnold left the bench. Catherine took Lillian to the restroom, and I turned to stretch. The seats were all full in the public section, and there in the back row was Carlos, who raised his fist on his good arm like the winner in a prizefight.

CHAPTER THIRTY-TWO

I walked back to Carlos. "What are you doing here?"

"I wanted to see the big show that's kept us from seeing each other lately. I sure hope you never cross-examine me. You are one scary lady," Carlos said.

"Thanks for coming. I need all the moral support I can get." I waved as I went back to the defense table.

Lillian and Catherine returned to their seats. I explained to Lillian that Maddie Rodriguez was missing, and would not be testifying.

"That's good for us, isn't it?" Lillian asked.

"Yes, I think it is," I answered. Lillian continued to look composed and calm. I wondered if she was still taking tranquilizers. "Lillian, remember to write down anything you think is important during any of the testimony." I pushed her yellow pad back in front of her and noticed that so far there were only circular doodles on it. Too bad I'm not a psychologist and can read what they mean, I thought.

Judge Arnold reappeared. "Call your next witness, State."

The State called Dr. Sandra Wilson, a deputy medical examiner. She had a reputation for being an excellent witness and a straight shooter. She was sworn in and took her seat, unfolding a page of notes and removing some slides from an envelope.

I leaned over to Lillian. "This testimony may be gory. If you feel you don't want to hear it, you can leave the courtroom, but it's probably best if you can stay," I whispered.

"I'll stick it out. Nothing could be worse than the way I found Gary," she said.

Dr. Wilson was stating her ample résumé and years of experience while Lillian and I whispered.

"Now, Dr. Wilson, were you the deputy medical examiner assigned to perform the autopsy on Gary Yarmouth?"

"Yes, that's correct."

"When did you first become involved in this case?"

"I was called to go to the Yarmouth residence in Coconut Grove on the afternoon of February 8th. I viewed the body in the bedroom on the second floor. Two of my technicians removed the body and the bloody coverlet on the bed where he was discovered. I made a drawing of the scene, after making a quick examination of the body. I noted the time to be four thirty-five p.m.

"Could you tell how long the victim had been dead?"

"Rigor mortis had not yet set in; that is, the body

was not stiff, although the victim was cool to the touch. Bleeding had stopped. It could have been a matter of hours. Not long though."

"What was your next involvement?"

"I returned to the office and completed my notes regarding the scene. I noted that the bedroom appeared to have been the scene of a struggle, a chair overturned, papers and books on the floor.

"I began my autopsy the following morning. May I put these slides on the viewer? They will help illustrate my findings."

"Any objection, Ms. Katz?" the judge asked.

"None, Your Honor."

Sandra left the witness chair and standing next to the large slide viewer, placed three slides that were blowups of the chest cavity of Gary Yarmouth. A fourth slide showed a wound that appeared to be to an arm.

"Please explain your findings," Karl said.

"The first thing I noticed was a small bump on the head of the victim. There was an iron headboard on the bed where the victim was found. I opined that he might have hit his head in a struggle.

Next, I observed some defensive wounds on both of the victim's palms. They were small cuts. The victim must have tried to fend off his attacker. I removed the clothing, which was covered in a great deal of blood. The blood tests showed it to be only that of the victim. I examined the clothing carefully and microscopically and found hairs belonging to the victim. However, there were two strands, which were long and blonde. They were clearly tinted that color as the roots were brown and the dye was apparent under the microscope. I bagged the hairs and sent them to the evidence lab.

Next I began the surgical examination of the organs. I found no traces of drugs or alcohol. The food left in the lower intestine was well digested and was ingested several hours earlier. The heart and chest cavity was the locus of the major wound."

Sandra pointed to the fourth slide. "This slide shows a wound to the right arm of the deceased. This wound is several centimeters above the defensive wound on the right palm. This wound is deep but clearly not deadly. However, it appears from the blood on the clothing I removed that it caused enough bleeding to have alarmed a victim. Perhaps the surprise or the pain from this gash would have stunned the deceased.

"The fatal wound is here." Sandra pointed to the large slide. "Here we have a puncture directly into the main artery that pumps blood to the heart. This wound was so severe that it caused death within a few seconds."

"What kind of instrument would cause such a wound?" Karl inquired.

"A knife or stiletto with a long, sharp blade. The blow would have to have been delivered with a great deal of force to pierce completely through, front to back. Additionally, the perpetrator thrust the weapon at the most opportune point to produce a mortal wound. The trajectory of the weapon bypassed the breastbone and other cartilage in the chest cavity, which allowed the knife to reach directly into the heart."

Sandra pointed to the two slides showing the heart from the front and the back. She pointed to a particular spot on the slide. "This is the point that a doctor probes with a long needle when a patient goes into cardiac arrest and it is necessary to enter the heart, thus bypassing those bony areas that I just explained." She pointed again to the darker areas on the slide. "The weapon used in this case made the same kind of entry directly into the victim's heart."

"Did you view other evidence in this case, Dr. Wilson?"

"Yes, you asked me to examine a silver letter opener. I measured the blade, which was exceptionally long. It measured over six and one-quarter inches."

"Could this letter opener have caused the fatal wound in this victim?"

"Yes, of course."

"Thank you, Dr. Wilson. Your witness, Ms. Katz," Karl said.

I looked up from my notes. Tears were running down Lillian's cheeks. Catherine had her arm around her and was pouring her a glass of water. I moved to the lectern.

"Dr. Wilson, you may take your seat again. Before we begin, I see that you are referring to some notes or reports. May I examine what you are looking at?" I asked. There was no objection from the prosecutors, who were in another conference with each other. No doubt they were still trying to locate Maddie.

"Yes, Ms. Katz. This is my summary report. It is a summary of my findings and notes in a short form," Sandra said as she held out the paper.

I took a minute to read the report. "Dr. Wilson, you have described the wounds, but you have not talked about where the perpetrator might have stood, based on the way the wound appeared. Have you formed any opinion about how the fatality occurred?"

"Yes, I have. It is my opinion that the person who committed this crime may have surprised the victim. He may have been asleep or resting. That may account for the bump on the top of his head. He may have sat up suddenly. The defensive palm wounds followed by the wound to his arm may have thrown him back on the bed. Finally, the fatal wound must have been struck with a great deal of force."

"What suggests this to you?"

"The weapon punctured the artery and left an exit cut on the victim's back. Additionally, the way the weapon punctured the artery in a straight-line trajectory shows that the perpetrator would have to have been standing above the victim, and would have to have been a tall individual to wield so much power.

The bed where the victim was found was a high, antique-type bed with an iron headboard, so a short person couldn't have maintained the velocity and power to inject such a straight path to the artery."

"Could the person have been on the bed with the victim?'

"It seems unlikely, as the victim was found on the edge of the bed facing the writing desk. According to the initial reporting officers, he had fallen to his side almost off the bed."

"Mrs. Yarmouth, would you stand up, please?"

Lillian looked at me with a frown and slowly stood up.

"Come around to the front of the table, please," I said. "How tall are you?"

"I'm five feet three inches," Lillian said.

"You seem taller. Would you remove the shoes you are wearing?"

Lillian stepped out of her black pumps. In her stocking feet, she appeared very small.

"Is Mrs. Yarmouth tall enough to have inflicted the wound the way you have described it?"

The medical examiner laughed. "I wouldn't think so unless she was leaping like a ballerina. And, by the way, I think Mrs. Yarmouth is stretching her height a bit. She looks more like five feet two inches. You know I measure a lot of bodies."

"Thank you, Dr. Wilson. I have no further questions. Oh, and here is your report. Thank you for letting me read it. I see that you have described in this report the way the wound was inflicted."

Karl Morris was on his feet. He didn't even bother to return to the lectern. From his table, he asked, "Ms. Wilson, you don't know that the defendant didn't murder her husband, do you?"

"I don't know who the murderer was, sir. I can only describe the facts that I found in my examination, but it's hard to imagine a woman that small making such a wound with that trajectory."

"You may be excused, Dr. Wilson," Judge Arnold said. "Call your next witness, Mr. Morris."

"Your Honor, the state has still not located Ms. Rodriguez. She was to be our last witness. If we do locate her, can we call her after the defense witnesses?"

"We'll cross that bridge when we come to it," the judge said. Are you ready with your first witness, Defense?"

"My paralegal is moving the witnesses to the courtroom area now, Judge. My first witness is Cassie Kahn."

"While we are waiting, let's take another short break. The court reporter looks like her fingers are sore."

CHAPTER THIRTY-THREE

The people in the public area pushed their way toward the door, heading for the restrooms and the coffee shop. Lillian stood in a circle with Brett and Sherry. I looked back to smile at Carlos when I spotted Jason Jimenez-Jones, the elected state attorney. He was sitting several rows back, blending with the rest of the peanut gallery. He must be here to spy on his assistants and make sure they don't cause him bad headlines, I thought.

I actually liked and respected Jason. I worked on his election campaign because I believed that he would be fair to my clients. Now I felt disappointed. Nothing had been fair about the case against Lillian. The State had stonewalled discovery and had filed the heaviest charge against Lillian with a threat of the death penalty.

I strolled back to Jason. He stood up as I approached. "Well, Mary, are the fireworks about to begin?" he asked.

"I'm glad you're here, Jason. You can hear first-hand how your office has screwed up." I smiled and moved back to where Carlos stood. I needed a reassuring hug, which I got along with, "Go get 'em, tiger. I'll be right here cheering, but quietly, of course."

Catherine returned in minutes with Cassie in tow. Cassie had done herself up to perfection. She was dressed in a black designer suit, a white sheer blouse with a low-cut neckline, and a small diamond pendant on a gold chain. Her hair was newly cut in a shiny rounded style. I hoped her testimony was as good as her appearance. Judge Arnold looked down approvingly from his vantage point on the bench as Cassie settled herself in the witness chair. He seemed fixated on the cleavage.

"Ms. Kahn, where do you live?"

"On Bayshore Drive in Coconut Grove."

"Do you know the Yarmouth family?"

"Yes, we've been neighbors for at least fifteen years."

"Do you see Lillian Yarmouth in the courtroom?"

"Sure, she's right there, next to the girl who brought me into the courtroom, and there are her children, Brett and Sherry, in the row right behind her. Well, they're really not children anymore, but you know, we always think of them as children."

I interrupted her. My instructions to just answer the questions must have made no impression on her. "I want you to think back to the day that Gary Yarmouth died. Do you recall that day?"

"Vividly. So much happened."

"When did you first see Lillian that day?"

"It was in the morning. She was in her garden and I went over to invite her to our house Sunday evening for cocktails. She told me her kids were coming home for the weekend from college. She was very excited and happy. She was such a devoted mother."

"Did you see her any more that day?"

"Yes, I was sunning by my pool in the afternoon when I saw her drive into her garage. I noticed how nice her Lexus looked. I waved, and she waved back."

I removed a photograph from the envelope and showed it to the prosecutor.

Karl stood up. "I object to this, Judge. I don't even know what it is. It's houses and yards."

I took the picture from Karl and showed it to Judge Arnold. "This is a layout of the Kahn home, the Yarmouth home, and the street in front of the houses. It's relevant to Ms. Kahn's testimony."

"Okay, Counsel, the clerk may mark it into evidence," the judge said.

"Now, Ms. Kahn, do you recognize what is in this photo?"

"Of course. There's my house and the pool, and here is Lillian's house and driveway, and there's our street. See, you can see how I had a bird's-eye view of their house from my pool."

"When you saw Lillian drive into her garage, do you know what time it was?"

"Yes, right after I saw her I looked at my watch, and when I saw it was already three o'clock, I was pissed. Excuse me Judge," Cassie smiled at Judge Arnold, "I mean, I was angry."

"What were you angry about?" I asked.

"The caterer who was doing the Sunday party was supposed to call me at two thirty so I could give her a final headcount and she could tell me if she was able to get all the seafood I had ordered. You know how scarce stone crabs have been lately. Well, I guess she thought I should just sit there and wait all day for her to call, so that's why I was angry."

"What happened next?"

"Well, I stood up to go in the house and call the caterer, and just then I saw a woman running down the sidewalk from the Yarmouths' house toward our house. She stopped for a couple of seconds right in front of our yard and stepped out of her shoes. They were those high wedges. I think they're by Remeau. Anyway, they're hard to run in, so I guess that's why she took them off and she ran down the street to a little red BMW parked in front of the house on the other side of my house."

I removed the photos of Maddie from the envelope and showed those to Karl. He looked startled.

"Any objection, Mr. Morris?" the judge asked.

Karl passed the photos to the other prosecutors, who looked at them and passed them back to me as I waited at the end of their table.

"I guess not, Judge."

The clerk marked the photos and I placed them on the arm of the witness chair.

"Ms. Kahn, would you look at these photos and tell me if you recognize the person in the photos?"

"This looks like the woman who ran down the street that I just told you about. The thing that is so distinctive about her is that reddish-blonde hair. What a gorgeous color."

"Can you show us on the photo of your house, exactly where the woman stopped? Just put an X there with this pen." Cassie marked a space in the first photo, just in front of her house on the sidewalk.

"Do you recall anything else about that day?"

"Well, later my maid came and told me that there were police cars and an ambulance next door. Then a young officer came to the door and asked me about the stuff I just told you, and then later on I went outside to see what had happened. A lot of the neighborhood was standing out there. They said Gary was dead. And then we saw the police lead Lillian out of the house in handcuffs. It was unbelievable."

"Did the police or the prosecutor ever contact you again?"

"No, none of them did. The only person who contacted me was you."

"Your witness, Mr. Morris" I said. I hoped that Cassie would give shorter answers to Karl, but I didn't hold out much hope. She was enjoying her role way too much.

"Ms. Kahn, good afternoon. I'm Assistant State Attorney Karl Morris. I'm going to ask you a few questions on behalf of the State."

"I know how it works, Mr. Morris. My husband's a lawyer and I watch all the *Law and Order* shows on TV."

"Ms. Kahn, you said these photos look like the woman you saw. Are you sure it's the same person?"

"What makes me think it is, is the hair. I'm always observant of hair. I used to be a stylist years ago, before I met my husband, and that's really a great color job."

"But you can't be one hundred percent sure?"

"Well, if it's not the same person, there's some colorist who is getting that distinct color, and I sure would like to make an appointment with her." The audience laughed, and Cassie smiled at the judge, who smiled back before he went back to concentrating on her neckline.

"You don't know who this woman is, do you?"

"No, I don't know her."

"You've lived next door to the Yarmouths for a long time. Did you ever see them argue or fight?"

"No, everyone knew they were a great couple. They traveled a lot together and played golf and went out on their boat. They always seemed to be having fun. Gary was a fun guy, always telling jokes, and Lillian hung on everything he said. They always looked like an ad in a magazine, so attractive."

"Okay, nothing further, Judge."

"No redirect, Judge. I smiled at Cassie as she left the courtroom.

"The defense calls Jonathan Katz," I said, motioning to Catherine. She hurried out the door with the bailiff, who was feeling cheated out of his job of ushering in the witnesses. They both returned a minute later on either side of Jonathan. The clerk swore him in and he took his seat in the witness chair.

"Will you state your name and occupation, please?"

"Yes, I am Jonathan Katz. I am a board-certified attorney in the field of estate planning and probate law."

"Are you and I related?"

"Yes, I am your sister. I mean you are my sister. I am your brother. Excuse me Judge. I'm not used to being a witness. I usually ask all the questions," he said. Laughter rippled from the audience.

"Are you acquainted with the Yarmouth family?"

"Yes, I was Gary Yarmouth's attorney, and through him, I met the other members of his family over the last several years."

"Are you the attorney responsible for drawing Gary Yarmouth's will?"

"Yes, that's correct."

"After Gary's death, did anything unusual happen regarding that will?"

"Shortly after his death, a young woman came to my office, unannounced and without an appointment."

I retrieved the photos of Maddie from the evidence table and showed them to Jonathan. "Do you recognize the woman in these photos?"

"Yes, that's the woman who came charging into my office. Her name is Maddie Rodriguez."

"Your Honor, I respectfully request that your prior ruling regarding hearsay be in effect during the testimony of this witness. Ms. Rodriguez has absented herself from this court proceeding and is still unavailable," I said.

"Any news of your missing witness?" the judge asked Karl, who shook his head 'no.' "Yes, my ruling still stands, Ms. Katz. Proceed, please."

"Now, Mr. Katz, had you had any prior contact with this woman before she came to your office?"

"She phoned my office a day before she came there in person. She asked if I was the lawyer who had Gary's will. I told her I was. She told me her name and stated that she was a beneficiary. I told her that was incorrect. She became irate and called me a liar. I suggested that if she had some proof that she was mentioned in Gary's will, she should produce it, and I further told her she should hire an attorney to represent her."

"When was the next time you heard from Ms. Rodriguz."

"That was when she appeared in my office. I was in a client conference, but I could hear her shouting at my secretary. She was demanding to see me. I escorted her into a conference room. She began shouting obscenities at me and demanded to see Gary's will. I told her it would be made public in a few weeks and she would see for herself that there was no mention of her. She must have believed he was going to provide for her, because she just wouldn't quit screaming at me. I finally threatened to call the police if she didn't leave. She said I was going to be sorry."

"Did you take that as a threat?"

"Oh, yes. I had a meeting with our security officers in the building and told them not to let her into my offices again. Her temper was out of control."

"When was the last time you had worked on Gary's will?"

"In December he revised his will for tax purposes, putting their home and other real estate in Lillian's name instead of their joint names. He said he wanted to be sure that Lillian and his family were protected. He placed some of his investments in the trust he had created for his children."

"Thank you. Your witness, Mr. Morris."

Karl moved to the lectern with the yellow pad he had been writing on. "Mr. Katz, it's a fact that Maddie Rodriguez did not benefit from Mr. Yarmouth's death, correct?"

"Yes, but it's clear she didn't know that."

"Just yes or no will do, sir," Karl said.

"Objection, Judge. The witness is allowed to explain his answer," I said.

"Objection is sustained. The witness's explanation remains in the record."

"Lillian Yarmouth benefited greatly when her spouse died, didn't she?" Karl was becoming snide.

"Not really. She and her husband owned the real estate jointly, so she would have had all of it anyway when he died. It just lessened the inheritance tax consequences for future generations."

"Well, didn't she get everything when he died? Insurance, investments?"

"No, the insurance and investments went to the children. Lillian owned the controlling interest in the stock in Elite Wines, and she had a good deal of money of her own left to her by her father."

"May I have a moment, Your Honor, while I confer with co-counsel?" Karl asked.

The judge nodded and Karl and his underlings whispered for a few minutes.

Karl returned to the lectern. "You love your sister, don't you, Mr. Katz?"

"Sometimes." The audience chuckled and the judge laughed out loud.

"You were instrumental in getting the defendant to hire her, weren't you?"

"I made the introduction, but the choice of a lawyer was up to Mrs. Yarmouth."

"Well, it didn't hurt to have your recommendation, did it?"

"No, it didn't."

"And you'd like to see her win this big case wouldn't you?"

"Listen, Mr. Morris, I've been practicing law in this county for eighteen years. I am an officer of the court, and I think you are insinuating that I would lie to help my sister. Neither she nor I would permit such a thing." Jonathan's scowl turned his placid face into a thunderstorm. He almost never lost his temper, but when he did, everyone with a brain got out of his way.

"I'm done, Judge." Karl sat down.

"Redirect, Ms. Katz?" the judge asked.

"Yes, Your Honor. Mr. Katz, I didn't go over your résumé when you took the stand, but I need to ask you about your background. Did you graduate from law school with any honors?"

I graduated from the University of Miami School of Law, magna cum laude, and I received a special award for rewriting and helping enact a new honor code that is still in use today."

"Have you received any awards during the time you've practiced law other than passing your board certification?"

"Yes, I received the Supreme Court annual pro bono award for representing, at no cost, all of the occupants of the Baptist Home for the disabled and aged. Most of them had no opportunity to have wills leaving their personal effects to loved ones. My office drew wills for over forty of the elderly. I also received an award from Lambda Legal Defense for representing several young men dying of AIDS. I assisted them in readying their estates and made sure that their partners received the bequests that were legally left to them. This was also with no fees charged. There have been others. Do you want me to continue?'

"No, I think this clearly shows your reputation as an attorney," I said, as I moved back to the defense table. Jonathan left the witness chair, and I saw him sit down in the back of the courtroom with Carlos.

"The defense calls Bob Rose of the Rose Investigation Service," I said. Catherine and the bailiff paraded up the aisle and out the door again. In a few minutes they reappeared with Bob Rose. Rose looked like his name; a round placid face, sunburned to a florid color. Beneath the quiet manner were thorns just waiting to fend off anyone who challenged him. I almost licked my lips. He was the perfect witness to illustrate the lack of investigation of this case.

Rose gave a loud "I do" to his witness oath and took his seat. He opened his briefcase and removed his report, adjusted his glasses, and nodded his readiness to proceed.

"Please tell the court your name and occupation," I began.

"I am Robert Rose. I own and operate the Rose Investigation Service, which has been in business since nineteen eighty-one."

"Were you ever consulted in your capacity as a private investigator by Gary Yarmouth?"

"Yes, that's correct."

"When did you first meet with him?"

"It was December twenty-third. He came to my office and retained me to investigate the background of a woman employed at the Omni Hotel named Maddie Rodriguez. He also wanted us to give him a report on her activities. He believed she was stalking him."

"Objection." Charlene Montavo, third in command for the state was on her feet, shouting. "This is all hearsay, Judge."

"This clearly falls under the exception of unavailability. You can't be more unavailable than when you are dead," I said.

Karl tugged on Charlene's jacket, pulling her back to her chair.

"Objection overruled," Judge Arnold said. He was sitting forward in his chair, his pen poised over his notepad. He was definitely interested in this witness.

I retrieved the photos of Maddie again and showed them to Bob Rose. "Do you recognize the woman in these photos?"

"Yes, that is the woman that we began investigating on December twenty-seventh and continued to check on her activities until February second or third of this year."

"I am showing the State a copy of your report dated this February. Did you author this report yourself, sir?"

"Yes, I wrote the report and turned it over to Gary Yarmouth."

"Was this report made in the ordinary course of your business, and has it been in your possession since it was written?"

"Yes to both questions. I always maintain the original report and send a copy to the client for whom the report was made."

The prosecutors were engrossed in reading the report. Karl Morris looked pale. He would have looked worse if he had realized that the big boss, Jason, was watching at the back of the courtroom. "No objection at this time, Judge," Karl said.

"Now, Mr. Rose, tell us what you learned from your surveillance of Ms. Rodriguez," I continued my questioning.

"We followed her in her automobile on the evenings of December thirtieth and thirty-first to the Yarmouth residence. She parked across the street. We observed her watching the house with binoculars. She also made calls on a cell phone. On the thirty-first she followed the Yarmouth automobile, a Lexus SUV, to a yacht club. She tried to enter the parking area of the club, but was turned away by security."

"Did you note what kind of car she drove?"

"Oh, yes, she drove the same car on all the occasions that we surveilled her. It was a 380 BMW, color red, Florida tag H 38 DC. We observed her on ten other occasions outside of the Yarmouth residence during January and February. On January thirtieth she went up to the residence and placed something in the mailbox at one thirty p.m. On February second, we observed her entering a condo building in Miami Beach at fifty-eight-oh-one Collins Avenue. The Yarmouths own a condo in that building. She entered the building around eleven a. m. and returned to her car at twelve forty-five. There was no doubt that she was stalking Gary Yarmouth and his family."

"You stated that you were also requested to investigate the background of Maddie Rodriguez. Did you author a report on her background?"

"Yes, we performed a thorough background check, and interviewed various witnesses, and checked documents where indicated."

"Tell the court what information you uncovered."

"We verified that she was a graduate of Florida International University. We verified her employment with the Omni Hotel Corporation. We also verified that she had been married briefly to a Joaquin Serrano in 1997 while they were both students. They were divorced that same year. We were unable to find Mr. Serrano. He had not been seen or heard from by anyone since their divorce.

"We learned that Maddie had resided with Bertram Olensky, manager of the Omni hotel in Ft. Lauderdale. This was in 1999. Mr. Olensky was sixty years old at the time and had just divorced his wife. Mr. Olensky disappeared in 2001. He had tendered his resignation to the hotel by letter and with no notice. We interviewed his ex-wife. She had not heard from him since 2001, and had been searching for him as he owed her a great deal of alimony.

"In 2003, Maddie had an affair with Morris Meier, a vice president of Ross Food Distributors. We located Mr. Meier who was now living in another county in Florida with his wife. He stated that he had terminated the affair after a few months, and was apprehensive about Maddie finding him. We noted that he described her as unstable. She had informed his wife of the affair and both had observed her uncontrolled temper."

"Did you meet with Mr. Yarmouth at any other time?"

"I met with him again in my office on February third, and went over some of the points in my report that I sent to him a day later. I suggested he call the police and get a restraining order against her and seek stalking charges against her. He said he couldn't do this without causing a scandal, that he loved his wife and wouldn't want to end his marriage, and that he would have to cut his losses somehow. He said he would pay Maddie off, if necessary."

"Thank you, Mr. Rose. I have no further questions," I said as I took my seat. I looked over at Lillian, who was crying. Catherine handed her more tissues. Sherry was leaning over the railing, patting Lillian's shoulder. She was crying, too, but Brett sat stone-faced, staring straight ahead. I was glad that I had decided not to call him as a witness. He would be dealing with his anger for a long time.

Karl carried the Rose report with him to the lectern. He looked at it as if it were a snake preparing to bite him.

"Good afternoon, Mr. Rose. My name is Karl Morris. I have some questions on behalf of the State."

Mr. Rose nodded, and settled deeper into the witness chair.

"You testify in court a lot don't you, sir?"

"Yes, it goes with my profession."

"So it would be fair to say you are a professional witness. Correct?"

"I'm a professional investigator, licensed by this state. Along with that goes the responsibility to make my findings known in court."

"Isn't it a fact that your reports are slanted toward the findings your clients want?"

"I don't understand your question, Mr. Morris."

"Well, you charge a hefty fee for your services, don't you?"

"Not as hefty as lawyers charge." Once again, the audience laughed.

"How much do you charge?"

"Generally, fifty dollars an hour, and a retainer fee of five hundred dollars. If I have to travel out of town, I charge for air fare and other travel expenses."

"How much did you charge Mr. Yarmouth?"

"Just a minute. I will look at his bill." Bob Rose opened his briefcase and pulled out a folder. He glanced through it, pulled out a paper, readjusted his glasses, and began to read. "Hourly fees, thirty-five hundred dollars, retainer fee five hundred, expenses and copying one hundred ten, total forty-one ten."

"You want to be sure your customers are satisfied after spending so much money?"

"I want to be sure that I do a complete job."

"So it's true, isn't it, that you slant your report in favor of what your client wants to hear?"

"Mr. Morris, my clients are usually unhappy when they hire me and more unhappy after I finish my report. I am hired in many divorce cases where I have to tell my client that their spouse has exactly the amount of money he says he has and has not been unfaithful. On the other hand, I often have to tell the wife who hires me that her husband is cheating on her. The truth very often hurts my clients. Mr. Yarmouth was certainly not a happy camper when he found out that Maddie Rodriguez was hanging around his home."

"Now, Mr. Rose, did you contact the defendant or the defense attorney after Mr. Yarmouth's death?"

"No, I did not."

"Then how did defense counsel have access to your report?"

"I guess she just did a better investigation into this case than you did."

"You've never investigated Mr. Yarmouth's murder have you?"

"No, I haven't."

"And you don't know who murdered Gary Yarmouth, do you?"

"I'm pretty sure it was Maddie Rodriguez. Two of her past lovers disappeared with no trace."

"Your Honor," Karl shouted, "I object to this witness speculating, and I ask for his last answer to be stricken."

"I can strike it from the record, I guess, but you can't unring a bell. I heard his answer," Judge Arnold said. "Maybe you shouldn't have asked him that question. Do you have any more questions, Mr. Morris?

"No, I'm done," Karl said.

"No redirect, and the defense has no further witnesses," I said.

"Then I will hear brief argument from each side, and I do mean brief," Judge Arnold said. "Defense, let's start with you. You asked for this hearing in order to show that there was no proof evident or presumption great that your client perpetrated this crime. Give me a short summary."

I got to my feet. It appeared that Judge Arnold didn't even want to hear from the State. Maybe he wanted me to pull together the facts for him in case he was ready to write an order.

"Judge, the State's own witnesses proved my point without my calling any witnesses, but I wanted to show the court the evidence that lay at their fingertips that showed my client's innocence if only they had investigated.

"The lead detective never talked to Cassie Kahn who saw Maddie Rodriguez running from the Yarmouth residence at the time of the murder. He never investigated whether Ms. Yarmouth had just come into the house. He could have followed up by checking with the car wash and the stores she had just visited. Instead, he relied on his 'gut instinct' to charge a grieving spouse with the murder of her husband.

"The medical examiner pointed out the fact that Ms. Yarmouth was an unlikely suspect because of the trajectory of the stab wound and her petite size. That's all the State provided to this court.

"As I said to this court previously, there is not one scintilla of evidence that points to Lillian Yarmouth as the killer. My witnesses point to another person, to Maddie Rodriguez, placed at the scene by Cassie Kahn. Maddie Rodriguez identified in pictures as running to the red BMW, which we know for sure was hers. Maddie Rodriguez, who believed that she would come into an inheritance from Gary Yarmouth. Maddie Rodriguez, who disrupted Jonathan Katz's law office, displaying her volatile temper. Bob Rose identified Maddie Rodriguez as a stalker, following Gary Yarmouth and lurking outside his residence on a dozen occasions leading up to his murder. And now, the worst two results of the State's failure to carefully develop this case are that my client has been wronged and shamed, and the real killer has now disappeared. I ask this court to dismiss this case against Lillian Yarmouth." I sat down, my hands sweaty and shaking. I looked expectantly at Harvey Arnold.

Judge Arnold looked at his note pad for a few minutes. Then he looked around the courtroom. Catherine passed me a note. "There's a lot of press here. Look around," the note said. I glanced behind me and saw that there were cameras and reporters all around the periphery of the courtroom.

Judge Arnold cleared his throat. "There will be a ten minute recess," he said. He bolted for the door leading to his chambers with his bailiff hurrying to keep up.

"The wimp," I said under my breath.

"What does this mean?" Lillian was squeezing my hand.

"It's hard to tell, Lillian. He's an inexperienced judge. He's probably calling another judge to ask what to do. I know it's hard to be calm, but let's be optimistic. I'm going to go thank our witnesses," I said. I went out into the hallway and shook hands with Bob Rose.

Jonathan and Carlos were standing beside me when I turned around. They took turns hugging me. Before we could say a word, Catherine came rushing out. "The judge wants to see all counsel in chambers right away," she said.

I hurried down the corridor leading to the judge's chambers. Several reporters were lined up along the corridor. They hurled questions at me as I ran by. All I could say is "I don't know." I couldn't believe that any judge would keep such a nonexistent case alive.

The four prosecutors were already seated around Judge Arnold's conference table. I sat down across from them, feeling like an orphan. They had each other. I was alone.

Judge Arnold was seated at the head of the table. He had removed his robe and hadn't bothered to put on his suit jacket. I noticed that the sleeve of his shirt was slightly frayed. Just the kind of thing my mother would notice.

Judge Arnold poured a glass of water from a silver carafe and slowly drained his glass. He looked around at all of us. He took off his glasses and took a cloth from a drawer in the table. He rubbed the lenses several times, put the glasses on the table, rubbed his hands together, and finally began to speak.

"The thing of it is, I've been told that it's up to the State to drop this case. They filed it and it's their responsibility," he said.

I was right. He had called a recess in order to talk to another judge, who must have been as big a wimp as he was.

"Judge Arnold, in a case like this where the State intends to proceed with no evidence against my client, you would be totally justified in dismissing the case. If you give me a few minutes, I will show you other cases in which the court has been upheld in similar dismissals," I said.

"Ms. Katz, I agree that there is no showing of evidence by the State today, but it's their burden to correct their mistakes, so I want the State to take the appropriate action." Judge Arnold picked up his glasses and began cleaning them again.

"Judge, I am just an assistant state attorney. I can't take that action on my own. It will take me some time to consult with the head of major crimes in our office and with the state attorney," Karl said.

"Karl, your boss, the state attorney, Jason, has been in the audience listening to this hearing all afternoon. Surely, you saw him there. Why can't you consult with him right now?" I said.

I couldn't read from Karl's expression whether he knew Jason was there. He was trying to bide his time and stall as long as possible.

"Go out and see if he's there, Mr. Morris, and ask him to come in here," the judge said.

Karl left. Charlene Montavo tried to go with him, but Karl told her to stay put. We chatted about the weather: another beautiful Miami winter; the Florida Panthers Hockey Team: another disastrous season; the amount of traffic around the courthouse: an incurable problem. Then we all fell silent. My nerves were stretched as taut as a trampoline. I could only imagine how scared Lillian must be.

After an interminable silence, Karl reentered the room. Slightly behind him was Jason Jones. Slightly behind him was the court clerk. Jason was carrying several sheets of paper.

"Good afternoon, Judge Arnold," Jason said. At this time, I have prepared a nolle prosse of this case. We cannot in good conscience proceed against Lillian Yarmouth, and it's not my intention to do an injustice. We relied on the homicide detectives to do a thorough investigation. It's clear that has not been done. I brought the clerk in with me so she can certify this dismissal of prosecution and conform the copies which I will give to Ms. Katz."

"Thank you, Jason, for doing what's right," I said as I extended my hand.

Jason shook my hand. He looked at me and continued, "But I want to warn your client that I can refile charges against her at any time if evidence is developed that would allow me to do so. There is no statute of limitations for murder. Of course, my office will take over an investigation into Ms. Rodriguez. If we find her, I will hold her as a material witness who has violated her subpoena and fled the jurisdiction of the court."

"Thank you, Mr. Jones, for acting in a responsible manner," Judge Arnold said. "You are all excused." Relief flooded his face and he smiled broadly.

What he really means is thanks for getting me off the hook, I thought.

As I started toward the door, Jason laid his hand on my arm. "Mary, I want to speak to you for a few minutes." He looked like a thundercloud before a hurricane.

"Sure, Jason. Just let me go tell my client about this dismissal. I'll meet you right outside the courtroom."

CHAPTER THIRTY-FOUR

I waved the dismissal paper in the air as I returned to Lillian and Catherine, who had been joined by Jonathan and Carlos. Lillian, Brett, and Sherry hugged each other. Sherry was laughing and crying.

"I would like to take you and Jonathan and whoever else is here with you to dinner," Lillian was smiling. "I'll never be able to thank you enough," she said.

I explained that I had some last things to clean up with Jason and would meet them a little later. I told Carlos and Catherine to follow Lillian. "I'll be there in a little while." I waved cheerily and went to find Jason. I wasn't looking forward to having him spoil my glorious victory.

Jason was waiting for me. He steered me into the attorney's room down the hall, avoiding the media frenzy gathered near the elevators.

"Well, Jason, what is it? I asked as we sat down at the conference table. I don't suppose you're going to apologize to me and Lillian."

"Listen, Mary, I just want to set the record straight before you go out there and ream out the whole police department to the press. If that is your intention, I think you need to see the whole picture. Do you know how many murders happened in the city on the same Friday night of Gary's murder?"

No, I don't know that."

"I didn't think so. There were four other murders that night. One of them was a twelve-year-old boy who was killed by drug dealers. There was a drive-by shooting in Little Haiti, where a father and his daughter were gunned down for no apparent reason. And that was the same night a five-year-old little girl was found dead in a Dumpster five miles from her home. She had been raped, as well. Now put yourself in the shoes of the homicide unit. They had what they believed was a domestic argument gone bad. If you were in charge of the homicide unit, what would you investigate first?" Jason stopped and took a deep breath. He was as emotional as I had ever seen him.

"I understand what you're saying, but the Yarmouths lives were impacted, too, and—"

Jason held up his hand. "Just hear me out, please. Are you aware that the police department has had to cut back the number of detective positions due to a shortfall in the city budget? For the whole city, they now have only ten full-time homicide detectives and two borrowed from the gang unit. When the media interviews you, I don't suppose you could tell them that if the city doesn't get more money, the police have no chance of operating effectively."

"I understand what you're saying Jason, but that doesn't excuse the failure of your office to do its own investigation. You know I wanted you to be elected to your position. I believed you were fair minded."

"I'm not excusing my office either and I intend to do a lot of retraining after this case. Our prosecutors are overrelying on the police investigations, but you know how many lawyers we lose every year because of the low salaries here. That means that inexperienced prosecutors are promoted to higher positions before they're ready. It all comes down to money."

"Look, Jason, I'm not without sympathy for your problems, but the fact remains I had an innocent client whose family has been torn apart. The bottom line is every victim and every defendant deserve just treatment. You need to make your speech to community groups and to the legislature. My client will always be looked at as the woman accused of murdering her husband, and for that, someone should apologize to her. She's not going to try to sue you or the police in civil court for money damages. She doesn't need money. She just needs to rebuild her life. The next person who is wrongly arrested may not be so charitable."

"I promise you, Mary, I will bring my office up to speed. I hope we can still be friends. Thanks for letting me vent some steam."

"I'm glad you did. I feel better too." I gave Jason a peck on the cheek. He smiled. The cloud lifted from his face.

I left the courthouse by the side entrance and got to my car without talking to the reporters. I could forego my mother's phone call telling me how nice I looked on the TV news, but why didn't I do something about my hair.

I sped over to the steak house on Brickell Avenue where we indulged in a celebration. Sherry and Brett, Catherine, Carlos, and Jonathan were already into their second round of toasts when I arrived. Carlos ordered champagne and copious bottles of Argentine wine along with thick steaks. We ate and drank and laughed until my sides ached. And Lillian insisted on footing the entire bill.

After dinner, Carlos followed me home. I hugged Sam who celebrated that someone had finally come home to feed him. Then Carlos and I fell into bed and indulged in the best sex I can ever remember, in spite of the cast on his arm, and probably because of the champagne bubbles in my brain.

The next morning I actually slept until eight o'clock. Carlos was not in bed. I smelled coffee and found him struggling in the kitchen with his one good arm. The world looked magnificent. The sun glistened on the rosy ixora blossoms. Wild green parrots chattered at my bird feeder, undisturbed by Sam who was galloping around the backyard. The dog and the birds had learned to live in harmony, a sort of animal pact to keep to their own territories. I guess if people did that there would be no need for lawyers.

Carlos kissed the back of my neck, as I took over the breakfast preparations.

"We can take our beach weekend anytime you say," he said.

"When does your cast come off?"

"Next week sometime. And my parents' beach house will be empty for a few weeks. They are in Argentina visiting my brother. We can take Sam with us."

"So next weekend sounds perfect. I can't wait, but right now I have to get to work."

"Work? Today? I thought you'd take a day off."

"I need to catch up on all my other clients' cases, and I need to do some follow-up with Bob Rose."

"What do you mean follow-up? Lillian's case is over."

"There are some things that don't add up. I need to answer some questions, just for myself."

"Don't poke around too much. My grandmother always said 'What you don't see with your eyes, don't invent with your mouth.' I think it's a Spanish proverb, but it doesn't translate too well. You know what I mean. Don't second-guess yourself," Carlos said.

Catherine and I arrived at the office at the same time. She looked more disheveled than usual as she squinted in the broad sunlight. "I don't know about you, but I have a humongous headache. But I have brought my remedy with me, if you need it," she said.

"What kind of remedy?" I asked.

"Two parts tomato juice, one part club soda, one part bacon drippings, and a dash of Tabasco."

"I felt okay until I heard that recipe," I said. Some day soon, I just had to hear Catherine's story.

"Catherine, call Bob Rose right away and see if I can go see him some time today."

"What's up? Are you hiring him in another case?"

"No, I want him to set my mind at ease about this case. I want to know where Maddie Rodriguez is and how she managed to get away from here, among other things."

"Gee, Mary, I thought we were done with all this. I can't wait to hear what else is on your mind. This job is better than three soap operas."

"That's what I like, a happy employee. I was going to give you a bonus after this case, but maybe the soap operas are reward enough." We both laughed.

Catherine held out her hand. "I'll take the bonus. You are the best boss I've ever had."

CHAPTER THIRTY-FIVE

I met with Bob Rose that afternoon. He promised to get right to work on the questions I raised, and promised to work as fast as possible before more time faded any leads to Maddie and to whatever else surfaced about the Yarmouths.

I fell back into my familiar schedule of court dates, depositions, jail visits, workouts at the gym, and, of course, Carlos. He was becoming a permanent fixture in my life.

The anticipation of our beach weekend was better than the weekend itself. For starters, I was nervous about Sam destroying any of Angelina's crystal vases that adorned every table, or getting muddy paw prints on her white carpet. I thought I would die when Sam crawled up on the white silk sofa next to me, his shedding black coat leaving a jigsaw puzzle design.

Carlos kept assuring me that the cleaning crew would fix everything as soon as we left, but it was still hard to relax.

On Saturday evening, Marielena suddenly appeared at the door, which we had failed to lock. We were lying on the floor, arms and legs entwined when her bird-like trill startled us.

"Well, look at you lovebirds. I saw lights up here and thought your parents were back, Carlos," she said. She took a seat on the sofa, glanced at the dog hair, and wrinkled her nose. "Mary, we read all about your exciting case. Aren't you the clever girl, but don't you think she murdered her *esposo*?"

Carlos's face turned angry. "Mother told you that we would be using the beach place, didn't she? And Mary proved that Lillian was not guilty of any crime. Can I get you something, or are you on your way out somewhere?" He got up and took her by the arm toward the door.

"Oh, of course, I'm on my way to the club. I'll leave you two alone. Good-bye, darling boy," she said as she gave Carlos a kiss. She said nothing to me.

Carlos returned to the living room. Our mood was shattered. "I want to talk to you about Frank," he said. "Marco told me what happened at your house. I want to know why you couldn't tell me this yourself. Why do I have to hear from my cousin that you are in danger? I could kill that Wasp, Gringo Frank."

"That's exactly why I didn't tell you. I don't need you getting in trouble because of your Latin temper. I'm a big girl and I took care of things."

"Maybe you're still in love with that jerk, and that's why you didn't tell me."

"Oh, sure, Carlos, I'm in love with Frank, but I'm having sex with you every chance we get. Use your head. You know how I dislike Frank, and you know how I feel about you."

"If this is so, let's get married." Carlos sat across the room glaring at me.

"What a romantic proposal. You look like you'd like to slap me."

"I'm sorry, Mary. I want to make this relationship permanent."

"Carlos, it's just too soon. We are still getting to know each other. Some day this may be right, but not yet." I tried to sit in his lap, but he stood up and went to open a bottle of wine.

We came back to Miami the next morning. I dropped him at his house, and Sam and I went home.

CHAPTER THIRTY-SIX

Monday morning when I returned from court, Bob Rose was waiting for me. He and Catherine were at her desk drinking coffee and looking at an album of photos of wolves, a new addition to Catherine's collection.

"This is a nice surprise," I said as Bob and I shook hands. "Come into my office."

Bob settled across from me and opened his briefcase. He pulled out a folder and handed it across the desk. "You can read this when you get time. It's as much as I could find out. I'll give you the gist of it now, in case you think of anything else I can do for you."

I glanced down at the first page, which was titled "Information on the Disappearance of Maddie Rodriguez." I looked up. "Go ahead, Bob."

"Okay. I started at the Omni personnel office. The human relations director was reluctant to give me any information other than the fact that Maddie worked her last day on the Friday before your Monday hearing. However, I told her that the state attorney planned to subpoena all of their records as they were investigating Maddie as a person of interest in a murder. Somehow, I guess she thought I was an investigator with the State."

"My goodness, I wonder how she got that idea," I said. We both smiled.

"She said that Maddie had asked for an extended leave of absence; that she had a sick relative in another country, and had to leave immediately. Omni pulled her last pay check together quickly and she picked it up Friday afternoon and cleared out. The human relations gal thought maybe she had to go to Cuba, because she was so secretive.

So I sent one of my investigators, a good-looking young guy, over to the hotel where she had been working. He nosed around, pretending to be one of her boyfriends. The room clerk told him that Maddie said she came into some money and was going on an extended vacation. She tried to sell him her car, but he wasn't interested.

"Did he say where she got this money?"

"She told him that she made a good investment."

Just then Catherine appeared in the door. "I'm sorry to disturb you. Carlos is on the phone and he says it's important."

Bob nodded and stood up. "I'll go talk to Catherine for a few minutes," he said, and closed the door on his way out.

I picked up the phone. "What is it Carlos? Are you okay?"

"No, I feel terrible. I acted like a jerk. I just want to say I'm sorry. Can I come over later tonight?"

"Yes, of course. But right now I'm in the middle of a meeting. I'll see you at my house later." I hung up and retrieved Bob from the waiting room.

"Okay, we had just finished with what the room clerk had to say," he said as he glanced at his notes. "Next we searched the transfer of automobile titles at the DMV. We found a transfer of the BMW from Maddie to a Hilda Malaga. She lived in the building where Maddie had lived. Oh, we had already checked with the rental agent who said Maddie had broken her lease and paid the penalty of two months rent and forfeited her security deposit without blinking an eye; no argument at all.

"Hilda actually drove up in the BMW while we were knocking on her door. She said Maddie wanted to leave town right away and was willing to take a very reduced price for the car if it was cash. Hilda borrowed ten thousand dollars from her boyfriend, and Maddie turned over the car. She said Maddie didn't even take her junk out of the car and Hilda had to clean it out. She had the stuff in a shopping bag, which I took off her hands."

"Anything of interest in the bag?"

"Most of it was the usual, gas station receipts, a sweater, some earrings. Then we found a piece of paper which said 'meet L.Y. at eleven, fifty-eight-oh-one Collins Avenue, penthouse two, fifteenth floor.' That led me to look back to my original report to Gary Yarmouth. Remember when we followed Maddie to a condo building on Miami Beach, and someone let her in? She stayed almost two hours. It seems L.Y. could be Lillian Yarmouth. I always thought she might have met Gary there, or someone he sent to pay her off."

"Oh, my God. Remember when you saw Maddie put something in the mailbox at the Yarmouths? It was in the report you gave Gary. Well, Lillian told me she received an anonymous letter tipping her off that Gary was having an affair. I asked to see the letter, but she told me she threw it away. Is there more in the report?"

"We checked the airlines and found that Maddie left on Sunday before the Monday hearing on a flight to Madrid. She was using a passport from Spain. Is that a country that doesn't have an extradition treaty with the U.S.?"

"I don't know. I'd have to research it, but she could go anywhere from there. We may never know where she finally lights. I appreciate your doing this work so quickly. This report is confidential, isn't it? Just between you and me?"

"What report?" he said. I'm giving you the only two copies. I don't know what it all means, and I'm not sure I want to know." Bob closed his briefcase, and dropped his bill and some of his cards on my desk as he left.

I couldn't concentrate on anything after Bob Rose left. My mind whirled like a Cuisinart, grinding out one scenario after another. Finally, I packed my briefcase and left. I stopped at the market and picked up steaks and salad fixings. It had been a long time since I'd had the time or the inclination to cook. I even decided to splurge for the ingredients to bake a chocolate cake. Maybe it would be therapeutic.

By the time Carlos arrived, I had fixed an appetizing salad and marinated the steaks. The cake was another story. I ended up calling my mother to talk me through her recipe. She was ecstatic. Her daughter was cooking instead of visiting a jail. And she was cooking for a good-looking man. The cake looked a little weird, listing to the side, but it tasted good. I ate a slice just to make sure it wouldn't poison Carlos.

Sam announced Carlos's arrival by throwing himself against the front door. When I opened it, Sam almost knocked him over. I gave Sam a swat and Carlos gave me the kind of kiss that makes me forget about dinner.

Much later in the evening, Carlos grilled the steaks on my grill while I held the flashlight so he could see. We dug into the food without even polite conversation.

"What's on your mind? You're very quiet. Are you still angry at me?" he asked.

"No, it's not that at all. It's a worry about Lillian and the murder."

"I thought you were done with that. Don't tell me the State is filing new charges."

"No. It's what I found out today. I need to talk about this. In fact, I need your insight, but you can never tell any of this to anyone."

"Of course, I won't." Carlos looked pleased that I was confiding in him, and I felt it was a big step in our relationship. I had never discussed a case with anyone other than another lawyer.

"I asked Bob Rose to look into the disappearance of Maddie Rodriguez. She skipped out of town the day before the hearing on a plane to Spain, carrying a Spanish passport. She told one friend that she had come into money and was going to travel. She even sold her car for next to nothing."

"Sure she split in a hurry. She murdered her boyfriend," Carlos said.

"It's more than that. She left a letter in the Yarmouth's mailbox a few days before the murder. The Rose investigators saw her. When I told Lillian about Gary's affair the week before her hearing, I expected tears, shock, and anger. Instead she was calm and matter-of-fact. She said she knew about it; that someone had sent her an anonymous letter. She also said that this wasn't the first time he strayed from the home and hearth. But she said she loved him and knew he would never leave her because she was the one with the controlling stock in Elite Wines. Her father left her the biggest share of the stock."

"You mean the father left more of the company to Lillian than to her brother? You Anglos are a different breed. That would never happen in an Hispanic family."

"Oh, here we go with the macho stuff again. Do you want to listen?"

"Sure. Go ahead."

"When she told me that, I knew that Jack Brandeis hadn't killed Gary. There was a time where I actually suspected him. Lillian was the one he would want to do away with, if he wanted to run the whole company.

"Here's the kicker. Bob Rose found a slip of paper in Maddie's things she left behind. It said eleven a.m. L.Y. and the address of the Yarmouth condo on Miami Beach.

"Bob Rose wrote in his original report to Gary that Maddie was observed entering that building shortly before the murder. She stayed almost two hours."

"Maybe she and Gary were having a good-bye funch, you know, fuck and lunch."

"If that were the case, and Gary gave her some money, why would she kill him, and why would she come looking for an inheritance in Gary's will?"

"Okay, what do you think happened, Ms. Worrywart?"

"I'm afraid to think what I think."

"Now you sound like a Spanish *muchacha*," Carlos said.

"I think Lillian met Maddie at the condo, and they planned the murder together. She promised Maddie money to get out of town and that's the money that

Maddie said she came into. Maybe she actually believed that Gary was leaving her money too."

"Maybe Gary did give her money. You know there are other ways to arrange such things that have nothing to do with a will or any other legal document. Maybe Lillian had nothing to do with the murder or the money. She seemed so fragile when I watched her in court."

"I think it was an act that she's been using for years. She could have finally gotten fed up with Gary's running around on her and decided to play the grieving widow. She's a lot tougher than she appears.

"Look, Mary, we'll never know for sure, unless the State finally catches up with Maddie. After the lousy job they did in the case, it seems unlikely that they'll ever find her. Are you worried because you got Lillian off?"

"Not exactly. It's my duty to zealously defend my clients. It's not a matter of proving innocence. Not guilty is different than innocent. Not guilty means the government failed to prove its case beyond a reasonable doubt. That's the standard. That's the way our system works."

"So that's what you did. You showed the judge and the state that they had no proof to show that Lillian committed a murder. What's really bothering you about Lillian?"

"That she completely fooled me. I thought I was a better judge of people."

"Well, in spite of your façade of skepticism, you believe what people tell you. Look at the time you wasted on Frank. But this is what I love about you. Inside you're as soft as butter."

"You better never let anyone else know that or I'll get Marco to beat you up."

"Come on," Carlos said, let's leave these dishes and I'll show you how to forget all this worrying."

"I thought you already showed me."

"No, that was just a warm-up."

CHAPTER THIRTY-SEVEN

Two days later, when I returned from a deposition, Catherine handed me a message. "Call Angelina Martin."

Oh, oh, she's back and she found Sam's dog hair. I dialed her immediately. Then I hung up. Maybe I should call Carlos and find out what this was about, I thought. No, I'll face the music. I dialed her number again.

"*Oye*," Angelina answered. "I'm on the other line. Just a minute," she said.

"Okay, I'm back," she said after a wait of several minutes.

"Angelina, it's Mary Katz, returning your call."

"Of course, I know it's you darling. I have caller ID, you know."

"How was your trip? When did you get back? Thank you for the use of the beach house. It was a wonderful getaway."

"Yes, yes, you're welcome. We got back Sunday

night. It was fine. Now here's why I called you. You are one smart lady."

"Well, thanks. But why do you think I'm smart?"

"Remember when we were talking about my position on the board of directors at Elite, and I said Jack would be the new president and you said maybe Lillian would take over?'

"Yes, I remember."

"I thought you were just kidding, but you were right."

"What?"

"Today was the board of directors meeting to vote for the new president. Don't tell me you don't know."

"Know what?"

"Lillian walked in with almost all the votes. She had all her shares, and Gary's few shares he left to Beverly. You know, his secretary or assistant or whatever, and she voted for Lillian. Actually, Beverly nominated Lillian. Marian nominated Jack. Lillian and Beverly and one other member voted for Lillian and Jack conceded, so Lillian is now in charge of running Elite. And she made sure she was voted a nice big salary too. So you were right."

"Maybe she just plans to be sort of the ceremonial president," I said.

"Oh, no, she's picked out her office and she said she'd be announcing some new sales policies in a few days."

"How did Jack take it?"

"Marian told me on the way out to the car he'll probably retire in a few months. Anyway, who knew Lillian was such a hard-nosed lady."

"Yes, who knew? Thanks for letting me know, Angelina. I look forward to seeing you and J.C. again."

"You must come for dinner soon, darling. Ciao."

Well, that's Lillian's story. She's turned into an effective CEO. I went by to see her at her office, which looked like an ad in *Ms.* magazine. She was as calm as a regular Valium user even though phones were ringing, and employees were dashing in and out.

Brett and Sherry have returned to Dartmouth. Lillian told me that Brett is thinking about coming into the business, and Sherry is considering law school. She got turned onto it by her mother's case. And I received a case of Merlot from Elite Wines with a note from Lillian that she would be sending me more wines as new ones arrived.

So here I am back at the car wash waiting for my car. Like I told you at the beginning, I went to the car wash in February and I ruined my life. I mean I ruined my old life, I broke my engagement, I was fired, I was sued, and I got a bar complaint. On the plus side, I have a whole new life. I have my own law practice, I won a murder case, and, best of all, I have a sexy new boyfriend, even though he does have a Latin temper and an impatient streak.

The car wash is extra noisy today. I might as well not even open my briefcase. I wonder why the two young guys next to me on this bench are screaming at each other. Now they're running down the sidewalk and they're still screaming. I can't make out what they're saying. Something about cops. Now there are more guys chasing the first two guys. Oh my God, it's the SWAT team. They just handcuffed the two young guys.

"Hi, can I be of help? I'm Mary Magruder Katz. Here's my card. I'm a criminal defense attorney. Don't say anything to these cops without your lawyer present."